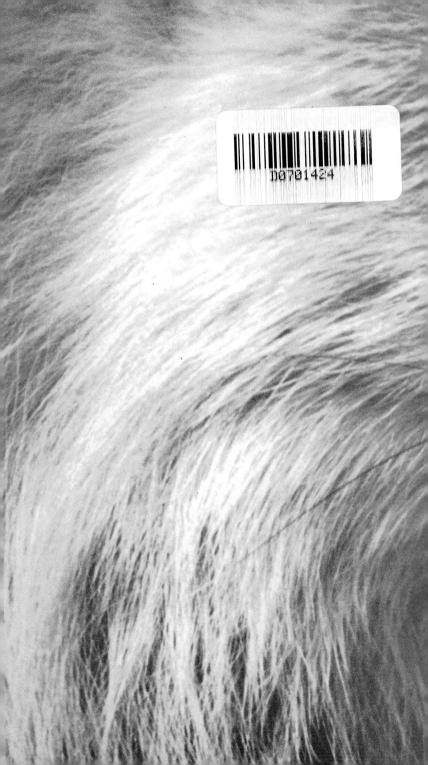

Foxed

Garry Ryan

FOXED

×

A Detective Lane Mystery

NeWest Press

COPYRIGHT © GARRY RYAN 2013

LIBRARY AND ARCHIVES CANADA CATALOGUING IN PUBLICATION
Ryan, Garry, 1953–
Foxed : a Detective Lane mystery / Garry Ryan.

Issued also in an electronic format. ISBN 978-1-927063-40-8
I. Title.

PS8635.Y354F69 2013   C813'.6   C2013-901572-8

Editor for the Board: Leslie Vermeer
Cover and interior design: Natalie Olsen, Kisscut Design
Cover photo: (Footprints) © Fancy Photography/Veer (Fox) © Johner Photography/Veer
Author photo: Luke Towers

Canada Council for the Arts   Conseil des Arts du Canada   Canadian Heritage   Patrimoine canadien

accessCOPYRIGHT FOUNDATION   Alberta Government   Edmonton   edmonton arts council

NeWest Press acknowledges the support of the Canada Council for the Arts, the Alberta Foundation for the Arts, and the Edmonton Arts Council for our publishing program. We acknowledge the financial support of the Government of Canada through the Canada Book Fund for our publishing activities.

#201, 8540–109 Street
Edmonton, Alberta T6G 1E6
780.432.9427
NeWest Press www.newestpress.com

No bison were harmed in the making of this book.

printed and bound in Canada

for
INDY,
ELLA
and
ISAAC

chapter 1

Lane sat on a bench, inhaled fresh Rocky Mountain air and smiled at the painting of reflected peaks on the surface of Lac Beauvert. He rubbed his right hand over his short brown hair and stretched his lean six-foot frame. A goose flapped its wings, accelerated, began to step lightly on the water and then rose into the air. He watched the bird's image and its wake ripple across the mountains reflected on the water. The evening sun made the lake's surface into sparkling diamonds and emeralds.

The food, the coffee, the mountain air. I haven't felt this relaxed in a long time, he thought. He wiggled his toes in his sandals and wiped at a speck of lint on his grey slacks.

"Shit!"

Lane turned.

Christine put one hand on the back of the bench, lifted her right running shoe and looked at the sole from over her shoulder. His six-foot-tall niece was wearing a white sleeve-less blouse, baggy white shorts and cream-in-your-coffee skin.

Lane looked around. Every male and every other female within shouting distance were looking their way. He could read their minds.

Christine dragged her shoe over the grass. "There's goose shit everywhere! How could geese have that much crap in them?" She looked out over the water at a Canada goose being followed by five goslings and cooed, "Awww. Do you see that? Aren't they cute?" Christine pointed at the family. She handed Lane his cell phone.

He stuffed it in his shirt pocket.

The invasive rumble of unmuffled exhaust pipes made them look left.

A pair of low-slung motorcycles approached along the road leading to the lodge entrance. Both riders wore black leather, ample bellies, sunglasses, tattoos and black helmets. The lead rider eased off on the throttle. The second rider spotted Christine.

The second rider promptly forgot about his front-running riding partner. There was a scream of metal. One engine raced, the other stalled and both bikes fell over. A second engine died.

The riders got to their feet in the sudden quiet. One looked hopefully in Christine's direction.

Christine looked at the wreckage. "What were they looking at?"

Lane smiled. "You."

"What's that supposed to mean? You think it's my fault?" Christine frowned.

Lane thought, *Quick, change the subject.* "Where are Matt and Dan?"

"Swimming." Christine looked over her shoulder at the pool. "You didn't answer my question."

Lane stood up. "No, I don't think it was your fault! You're drop-dead gorgeous and oblivious to the fact. Arthur's having a nap. If you get him, I'll get the other two and we'll go get something to eat."

The five of them met for dinner. The table overlooked the lake and the surrounding mountains tipped with white.

Matt had lost weight, was shaving every day and wore his black hair cut short. He said, "It would be nice to stay for a few more days."

Christine said, "You know, this is the first time I've been to Jasper. *And* the first time I've seen a grizzly."

Daniel, her brown-haired boyfriend, was taller than Christine, slender and introverted. He was finally beginning to feel relaxed enough around Lane to open up. "The grizzly was incredible."

Lane nodded. "It was a thing of beauty. A hunter." *It's good to be talking about bears instead of cancer, surgery, scarring, fatigue and what the last doctor had to say.*

"Okay, tell us what you're thinking." Arthur looked out over the water. His new exercise program was beginning to pay off. His belt had two old cinch lines in the leather to prove it. It hadn't, however, helped him grow back the hair atop his tanned head.

"I was thinking how it's good for all of us to be here. I was thinking I'm glad you don't have to have chemo. And I was thinking we should go to California next. Maybe San Diego." Lane looked around the table, gauging the reactions of four people.

"Can Daniel come?" Christine asked.

"Can we stay close to the beach?" Matt asked.

Lane's phone began to vibrate in his shirt pocket.

Arthur smiled. "That's not what I asked you. That's not what you were thinking. You just changed the subject again."

"You really want to know what I think of grizzlies?" Lane asked.

He felt their curiosity pique and the resultant attention shift in his direction.

Lane ignored his phone. "The bear was afraid of us, yet we fear it. It's a hunter. It's very good at what it does. And it makes us feel like prey. Still, we're not the endangered species."

"Like you," Matt said. "You're a hunter."

"And people fear you," Daniel said.

Lane picked the phone out of his pocket and flipped it open.

Christine grabbed it from him and put it to her ear.

"Hello?" She slapped Lane's hand away as he reached to take the phone back. "Hi, Keely. How are you? Yes, we'll be back tomorrow. Probably in the afternoon." She listened for a minute, then said, "I'll pass the message along. He's right here, but we were in the middle of a good conversation, and he was using your call as an excuse to avoid answering a tough question. You know how he avoids answering the questions he doesn't want to answer? I'll get him to call you right back."

"What's up?" Lane asked.

"I'll tell you when we finish this conversation." Christine curled her fingers around the phone.

"Could I have my phone back, please?" Lane motioned with his open right hand.

"No." She put the phone on the table, covered it with a napkin and put her hands over top.

Lane looked at Arthur, who was getting his spark back after a double mastectomy. It had been a long haul. There was the shock of the diagnosis, the operation and recovery from surgery, then the chemo and all of those lovely side effects.

Arthur said, "She wants some answers. You expect the same from us. Remember your big speech about us being honest with one another?"

"Okay. What do you want to know?" Lane refilled his coffee from the carafe at the centre of the table.

"Do you admire the grizzly because it's a hunter like you?" Matt asked.

"Or because it's feared and misunderstood?" Arthur asked.

"What about the fact that it's nearly extinct?" Christine asked.

Lane joined in on the laughter.

Daniel said, "Of course it's not because male grizzlies sometimes kill male cubs."

Christine glared at Daniel. "How did you know that was what the call was about?"

Christine will forever be leaping to conclusions after the way she was mistreated in Paradise, Lane thought, then asked, "About what?"

"Keely said they found the body of a missing boy. She thinks it may be related to one of your unsolved cases." Christine lifted the napkin and handed him the phone.

chapter 2

After breakfast, Matt and Christine insisted on sharing the driving duties for the five-hour trip home. Christine drove the first leg along the mountain valley parkway south to Lake Louise. For the most part, the two-lane highway ran between two mountain ranges. At one point, the road climbed up to the Columbia Icefield. Fresh snow on the mountaintops reminded them that even summer in the Rockies is temperamental. They reached Lake Louise, stopped for gas and then drove east, descending into the foothills. Matt drove the second leg.

Daniel and Christine snored with a wide-awake Arthur sitting next to Christine and the window. He listened to music with his eyes closed.

Lane closed his eyes and remembered the picture of Zander Rowe. The boy was eleven when he disappeared. He left school one day and never made it home. His older brother, Robert, was in jail at the time. Lane wondered if Robert was still inside. Lane closed his eyes and could see the faces of the father and the mother. Mrs. Rowe sat there quietly, numb with shock. The father went on and on about problems with the justice system. He kept saying, "Fuckin' cops," over and over.

"So, it was as you thought. Zander was dead before you even began to work on the case," Arthur said.

Lane nodded. "Looks that way. I wish you would stop your annoying habit of reading my mind." He turned in his seat so that he could see Arthur.

Matt checked the rear-view mirror.

"It's not all that difficult. Ever since you talked with Keely, you've had that look in your eyes." Arthur looked at Matt's eyes in the mirror and asked, "Are you sure you want to hear this?"

Matt shrugged. "I can drive and think at the same time."

Arthur chuckled. "That's not what I meant. Zander was eleven years old, and Lane couldn't find any trace of the boy. A couple of months after the boy disappeared, his older brother killed someone in prison. We both thought the disappearance and the murder were connected. It was suspected that the older brother had been involved in at least two drive-by shootings and two killings. Lane thought the younger brother was killed out of revenge for one of those gang killings."

"It's beginning to look like I was right," Lane said.

"Then where will you start?" Matt asked.

"First we have to be sure that the body is Zander's. Then we'll see if any of the original suspects are in some way connected to the location of the body." Lane looked out the window. They dropped into the valley. His ears popped, and he swallowed to equalize the pressure.

"The trail is ten years old," Arthur said.

"A body can change all of that with the evidence it provides," Lane said.

An hour later, they neared home. Matt turned off the main street. On their right, a sandstone retaining wall stepped up three levels — a stairway to the houses looking down on the rest of the neighbourhood. The stuccoed houses with red-tiled roofs were situated along the edges of a private eighteen-hole golf course.

"What's going on?" Christine asked, having woken up.

Four men pointed long-lens cameras at the rock wall. A row of cars was parked along the far side. Spectators faced the wall.

Matt slowed and stopped.

"What are they doing?" Lane asked.

Arthur tapped Lane on the shoulder. "Over there."

Lane saw a red fox approaching the rough of the golf course. It looked thinner than it should be at the height of the season.

The fox leapt up to the first level of the retaining wall.

"What's that in its mouth?" Christine asked.

"Looks like a gopher," Matt said.

Four kits appeared from crevices in the wall. While their mother looked emaciated, they looked plump with thick and fluffy red coats. Her coat was thinning to black on her haunches.

The mother dropped the gopher. There was a snapping of camera shutters. The kits went for the carcass and proceeded to rip it apart.

"How will the kits be able to survive here?" Lane asked.

Daniel said, "We're missing the obvious. The kits look like they're doing just fine. It's the parent who looks unlikely to make it to the end of the summer."

chapter 3

"Mochaccino?" Keely asked.

Lane took the cup, passed it under his nose and savoured the aromatic blend of coffee and chocolate. "Thanks. My turn next." He looked at the chain-link fence that surrounded the various police vehicles in the downtown lot.

Keely had her chestnut hair cut short and wore a navy jacket and slacks. She held out the car keys. "You wanna drive?"

"You drive. You've already been there." Lane walked around the rear of the Chev and got in the passenger side. "I like the new hairstyle."

Keely sat behind the wheel, flicked her fingers over the top of her close-cropped head and said, "I'm getting used to it." She started the car.

"Thinking of joining the Marines?" Lane put his seat belt on.

"Nothing like that." She put her seat belt on, put the car into drive and eased out of the lot, ignoring his attempt at humour.

Lane sipped his coffee and waited.

"Look, I'll explain the hair later. Right now I need to get you up to speed about Zander Rowe." Keely headed for Memorial Drive and away from the downtown core.

"Okay."

"The guy who found the room—where the body was found—moved into the building two weeks ago. He and his wife are starting up a brake and alignment shop." Keely shoulder checked before accelerating onto Memorial Drive and following it along the northern bank of the Bow River.

"What's his name?"

"Gordon."

Lane looked toward the river. Cyclists, joggers and walkers shared the paved paths on either side — well, shared it most of the time. When they didn't, an altercation would break out, and that thin layer of civility would peel away like plastic wrap covering spoiled food. "Can I work from this point on, then compare notes and impressions afterwards? That way I begin with fewer preconceptions."

"Sure." Keely pantomimed zipping her lips.

Lane met Gordon fifteen minutes later. Three thousand kilograms balanced over his head. He was working on a rusted pickup on a hoist. All four tires leaned against the wall.

Lane inhaled a mixture of grease, oil, brake fluid, gasoline and road dust. *Better than what I was expecting*, Lane thought.

Keely stepped through the office door on the upper level. She said, "Hello, I'm Detective Saliba," and closed the door behind her.

"Gordon?" Lane asked.

Gordon was working on a front rotor of the pickup. He turned, spotted the detective and said, "That's right."

"I'm Detective Lane." He studied Gordon's round features and the smile lines around his eyes. He was six foot four and more than two hundred pounds. *He's got arms like a weightlifter.*

Gordon turned and wiped his hands down the front of his blue coveralls. He wore a red ball cap with a Boston Red Sox logo.

Let's get this party started, Lane thought. "How did you find the room?" The detective glanced to his left in the direction of the stairs leading down to the lower level. The opening was taped off. He could see Dr. Weaver in his white bunny suit stepping out of a doorway. The doctor had a paper bag in his hand.

"An old friend came by a couple of days ago. He told me not to park any vehicles in the corner." Gordon pointed to a triangle of cement void of equipment.

"This friend's name?" Lane asked.

"I was told the information in confidence." Gordon crossed his arms.

You can protect your friend, for now. Lane asked, "How did he know about the room under the floor?"

"It's wired and plumbed. He did the job." Gordon lifted his chin.

"He told you this?"

Gordon shook his head. "No, he told me to look behind the sink. The rest I figured out on my own."

"How?"

"I've known him since high school. He's the kind of guy who does jobs under the table. People come to him because he works for cash. His specialty is electrical and plumbing. He lives in a house that's paid for. Likes to live a quiet life with few distractions." One of Gordon's eyelids dropped a little lower than the other.

"Hydroponics?" Lane asked.

"Yep."

"A little thieving on the side?" Lane asked.

Gordon gave Lane a practised blank look.

"So you checked behind the sink and found —?" Lane asked.

"There's a hole in the concrete. Behind that is an opening —"

"And?" Lane asked.

"There was a smell." Gordon looked at the floor.

Lane waited.

"It smelled of something old, something …"

"Dead?" Lane asked.

"Yes."

"So your friend worked for the former tenants?"

Gordon looked relieved. "Yes. They were evicted about six months ago. I moved in a couple of weeks ago."

"Did you know the former tenants?" Lane asked.

"Knew *of* them. They rebuilt classic cars but never had any vehicles parked out front. Were in business for eight years but never rebuilt a car." Gordon looked directly at the detective.

"How did you know this?" Lane asked.

Gordon smiled. "My old shop was two blocks north. I drive by here at least twice a day."

"So, you know the neighbourhood pretty well?" Lane asked.

"You might say that." Gordon planted his feet shoulder width apart.

"What do you think happened to the victim?"

"There were lots of rumours around the time Zander disappeared." Gordon looked over Lane's shoulder.

"Any one of the rumours make more sense than the others?"

"Zander's brother was in jail. It was common knowledge that Robert belonged to a gang and that he was involved in a few drive-bys before the kid disappeared."

"What are you saying?" Lane asked.

"Payback." Gordon frowned.

"Payback?" Lane waited. *Let him fill in the blanks for you.*

"Four guys were killed in those drive-bys. Every one of the guys killed had friends, family."

"You know these families?"

"No, but I went to school with some of the gang members. They had a kind of code. Mess with one of them and the others would come after you. Other than that, they're a great bunch of guys." Gordon looked in the direction of the office. "It was my wife's idea to call you guys, not mine."

Lane went to reply and stopped himself. *Leave an opening*

for the next time you talk to him. "Mind if I look at the room now?"

"Fine with me." Gordon turned around to work on the pickup.

As Lane stepped down to the next level, Gordon picked up an air hose and connected it to an air wrench. He stepped under the front end of the truck. There was a metallic click. Then the shop filled with the sound of exploding air and metal twisting off metal as the wrench loosened a bolt.

Down the stairs and inside the bathroom, the noise was muffled. Light shone through a hole chiseled out of the concrete wall. Lane crouched to look inside an opening that was, at one time, hidden behind the bathroom vanity. He caught a faint and familiar odour.

Dr. Colin Weaver — Fibre, as he was referred to — was an angel lit from two sides by portable lights, making his white bunny suit glow. He bent over a hollow in the gravel floor. Fibre used a trowel to work his way around the plastic the body had been wrapped in. Sensing Lane's presence, he turned to the detective and said, "I've got a headache."

"From the smell?" Lane asked.

"No, from the air tools." Fibre leaned his back against one of three walls that still had marks from the shovel blades used to dig the room. Even though his blond hair was stuck to his scalp, he still looked like he should be smiling from the cover of a fashion magazine.

Lane looked up at the rough underside of the concrete floor. Then he saw the outlet boxes for power, the pipes for plumbing, and asked, "Was this space ever used to grow weed?"

"I don't think so." Fibre sniffed for effect.

"How close are you to removing the body?" Lane asked.

Fibre did a mental calculation. "Once my assistants return, we should be able to remove the remains by this afternoon."

"Are you sure it's Zander Rowe?" Lane asked.

Fibre nodded. "There was an identification card. It was made of plastic and stuck inside a fold in the material the body was wrapped in. It has his name and school on it. We will still need to do tests. We have dental records. That kind of confirmation will take time. You understand?"

"I understand." Lane put his hands on his knees. "You'll keep me up to date?"

"As always." Fibre bent over the remains.

Lane heard the metal trowel scraping against stone. His spine shivered at the noise. He stood and looked at the light pouring out of the hole in the concrete.

×

"I got a name." Keely sat across from Lane at a picnic table. He'd just bought each of them a coffee at a shop next to Northmount Drive and close to 14th Street. Traffic produced a background hum.

Lane smiled. "The name of the guy who did the work on the plumbing and power?"

"That's right." Keely looked toward the west. "His name's Lionel Birch."

"How did you come up with a name?" Lane asked.

"I asked Louise," Keely said.

"Louise?"

"Gordon's wife. She runs the office." Keely swirled the contents of her cup.

Lane took a sip of coffee and watched the traffic rolling by. *How come you have big, dark circles under your eyes?*

"She's sick of him covering for his friends. Louise is worried the business might go under because of his so-called buddies and the investigation into Zander's death." Keely took a sip of coffee.

"What's up with you?" Lane asked.

"What do you mean?" Keely looked him in the eye, then glanced away.

Lane heard the wariness in her voice as the defences went up. "You're not yourself."

"Dylan moved out," Keely said.

"How come?"

"My dad's been after him for months — ever since we got engaged — to convert to Islam." Keely looked at the street as if something there could give the situation more clarity.

"And?" Lane glanced at her left hand. He saw that her engagement ring was missing.

Keely looked at Lane, focused on his eyes. "Dylan decided to convert. My dad was happy. I told them both to screw off." She spat out the last two words.

"I don't think I understand."

"Two guys get together and make this big decision. They take months to work it out and neither one asks what I think. Maybe Dylan's more like my dad than I thought. Anyway, I'm not devout. In fact, now that I've been thinking about it, organized religion has been a pretty shitty deal for women. You know, it's like what Christine said about her needing to be 'sweet' to fit in at Paradise. I was supposed to be *sweet* and go along with what the guys decided. It really pisses me off!" she finished. She'd been talking with her hands, and some of the coffee squirted out of the hole in the lid of her cup.

"I'm sorry."

Keely shrugged, licked the coffee of the back of her hand and said, "Dylan's staying with a friend. My dad can't understand why I'm pissed."

"What does your mom think?"

"She's so busy at work, she's hardly home. I haven't had much to say to her either. At least my brother is still talking to me." Keely looked east at a point in the distance.

✕

They found Lionel Birch at his home located on the flood plain near the Bow River on the west side of the city. He lived in a community called Montgomery, which used to be its own town before being swallowed up by Calgary.

Lionel was sitting on the back porch of his green bungalow, eating his lunch at a picnic table shaded by a purloined Starbucks umbrella.

Lane watched Lionel study them as they pulled up and parked across the street. The man looked to be around five and a half feet tall and wore a Blue Jays ball cap and at least two days' five o'clock shadow. He had one hand wrapped around a sandwich and the other around a bottle of Big Rock beer.

Lane and Keely walked side by side as they crossed the street and stood just outside the gate of Lionel's chain-link fence.

Lionel watched them with what appeared to be a lack of interest.

"I'm Detective Lane and this is Detective Saliba. May we come in?" Lane asked.

"Is this about Gordon's place and the work I did there a few years back?" Lionel set his beer down with exaggerated care.

Lane waited outside of the gate. *Don't get into a power struggle with this guy. Just answer his questions.* "Yes."

"Are you here to arrest me?" Lionel asked.

"Did you have anything to do with the abduction and murder of Zander Rowe?" Keely asked.

Good work, Keely, Lane thought.

Lionel shook his head. "No."

The detectives waited.

"Are you here to arrest me?" Lionel asked.

"If you had nothing to do with the abduction and murder, then we have no intention of arresting you." Lane put his hand on the gate.

"Come on in, then." Lionel stood up and indicated the detectives should sit across from him.

Lane and Keely sat down. The spruce bench boards of the picnic table creaked and groaned.

Lionel lifted his beer, smiled and asked, "Want a beer?"

Lane smiled back. *Lionel's a talker. So let him talk.*

"That job at Gord's shop was a cash deal. The room was dug when I got there. I just put in the flex pipe so they could move the sink in and out. Then I wired and plumbed the inside. It took four or five days, if I remember right. Of course it wasn't Gord who paid me to do that job." Lionel took a healthy bite from the sandwich, followed by a satisfying swig of Big Rock.

"Who paid you to do the job?" Lane asked.

Lionel smiled, put the beer bottle down and said, "Rather not say. Besides, all you have to do is check with whoever owns the building, and she'll give you the name. She's a widow. I can't for the life of me remember her name."

"We need the names of the former tenants," Keely said.

"Pretty bad for business if I start giving out the names of my customers to the police." Lionel wiped crumbs from his face with an open palm. "Considering the kind of work I do."

"Pretty bad for business if we pass your name on to Revenue Canada and suggest they audit you," Lane said with a smile. "Considering the kind of work *we* do."

Lionel took a thoughtful bite of his sandwich, chewed, covered his mouth and asked, "What do you want?"

"We want to know who killed an eleven-year-old boy and buried his body in the room you wired and plumbed."

Lionel rubbed his forehead like he was trying to rub away a headache. "I don't know nothin' about that."

"We need to know who paid for the room to be made hydroponically friendly," Lane said.

"It was a cash deal."

"Who paid you?"

Lionel looked around his backyard and then murmured, "Kev Moreau."

Lane sat back. *Finally, we're getting somewhere.*

Fifteen minutes later, as they drove downtown, Keely sat behind the wheel and said, "Moreau was a regular at the Scotch Drinkers' Club. Always very smooth. Always very charming. Always the centre of attention at any table. He loved to talk about architecture and his latest renovation project."

Lane turned to her. "Architecture?"

Keely nodded. "That's right."

"Surprising," Lane said. Then he added, "We need a meeting with Harper."

"How many restaurants does Moreau own now?"

"Five, the last time someone counted," Lane said.

"And they're all a front for his drugs?"

Lane nodded. "Among other things. He always keeps himself at arm's length from the illegal end of the business. Then he pays the legal costs of his managers or closes down whenever a bust is about to happen." *I wonder whether he was getting warnings from the Scotch drinkers?*

"Except for this time," Keely said.

"What do you mean?"

"He paid Lionel with cash." Keely eased the car right up close to the Bow River as they drove under a bridge.

×

Arthur was putting the supper dishes in the dishwasher when he said, "We need to go and pick up a prescription." He tugged up the waist of his pants and looked at Lane, who was holding his plate and a half-finished glass of beer. "I'll drive."

Lane felt the familiar grip of fear that tugged and tingled his elbows every time Arthur's health was mentioned. Arthur had lost weight, his hair was thinner and his Mediterranean skin was almost pale despite the summer sunshine. "Why do you need a prescription? Are you okay?"

"I'm fine. Remember? The surgeon said they got it all. The sentinel node was clear. The oncologist said the chemo worked. I was lucky."

Lane drained his beer. Roz's ears stood up.

Arthur had the car keys in his hand. "I'll explain on the way."

Within five minutes they were halfway to the grocery store. Arthur had his glasses on and had moved the seat forward so that his belly almost rubbed up against the steering wheel. They stopped at a major intersection where the light was extraordinarily long.

"Well?" Lane asked.

"Well, what?"

"Who's the prescription for?"

Arthur looked sideways at Lane. "Christine."

Lane waited.

"We went to see Dr. Keeler today. We dropped the prescription off and it's ready." Arthur checked the red light and looked away from his partner.

"Would you get to the point?"

"The doctor prescribed birth control pills." Arthur turned back to wait for the green light. Lane looked to his right. He saw a woman, a man, a baby stroller and a dog the size of a colt. The woman turned and talked to the white-bearded man. Lane noticed the woman's flat chest. *She's had cancer too. Now that I know what to look for, it seems it's everywhere.*

Arthur accelerated, turned left into the grocery store parking lot, parked next to a black pickup, shut off the car and got out. Lane followed.

"Come on." Arthur waited at the supermarket door. Again, Lane followed him inside.

"Daniel sleeps over. They've been together for how many

months? I mean, do I have to draw you pictures? Christine had a scare." Arthur grabbed a shopping cart.

Lane followed Arthur past the shampoo and headache remedies and stopped when Arthur picked up several packs of condoms. Arthur walked up to the pharmacy counter. "Prescription for Christine Lane, please."

The tiny dark-haired pharmacist turned, fetched the prescription, read it as she returned and looked confused. She stared at Lane and Arthur, also looking confused.

The pharmacist opened her mouth and closed it. She stapled the package shut, handed it to Arthur and said, "Use as directed." She waited.

Arthur paid for the prescription and dropped the package in the cart. "Come on, we need a few other things."

Thirty minutes later, they walked back into the house. Lane could hear Roz scratching at the back door. Lane asked, "Anybody home?" He looked at the shoes inside the door. He spotted Christine's running shoes and Daniel's black dress shoes.

Lane kicked off his own shoes and carried two bags of groceries into the kitchen. Arthur followed him and opened the fridge to put some fresh milk inside.

"Where are they?" Lane asked.

Arthur rolled his eyes. "Don't ask."

Lane sat down at the kitchen table. He put his head in his hands.

"Go out on the deck. I'll bring us another beer. By the way, there's something else."

"What?" Lane felt his defences going up.

"I've signed us up for yoga." Arthur ducked his head behind the fridge door as he reached inside.

"Yoga?" The word popped out even after he'd recognized the no-nonsense tone in Arthur's voice.

"It's part of the rehabilitation after cancer. Apparently the program is experiencing remarkable success. The first session is free to the survivor and a partner. Since you are my partner, I signed you up." Arthur raised his head from behind the fridge door and focused on Lane.

Lane recognized Arthur's I've-made-up-my-mind tone this time and, instead of responding, reached for the back door.

Roz pawed at Lane's knees as he opened the door. He saw Christine sitting in a lawn chair and writing in a journal. Daniel sat next to her on the deck, reading a graphic novel under the outdoor light. Lane stuttered, "But... I thought..."

Christine looked up at him. "You thought what?"

Daniel looked up, puzzled, waiting for Lane's answer.

"I'm tired. I think I'll go to bed early. Good night." Lane closed the door. He walked across the kitchen and to the stairs. There was a whimper. He looked left. Roz sat next to the front door. The leash was in her mouth and her amber eyes were on Lane. He stopped with his right foot on the first step.

"Shit." He turned to the dog, stuffed his feet in his shoes, attached the leash to Roz's collar and went out the front door.

Sensing his mood, Roz pranced along beside him, not pulling him along as she usually did.

In fifteen minutes, they found themselves across the street from the tiers of the sandstone retaining wall where two kits were visible in a nook and a cranny.

Roz studied the young foxes. One of them yawned. The other stood up. At this age the kit was round, like a stuffed toy, and it bounced rather than ran.

Lane looked at Roz and held the leash with both hands.

"What's up?" Matt called.

Lane turned.

Matt approached them. He was wearing shorts and a black T-shirt. He tried to catch his breath. "Uncle Arthur said you were upset."

Lane shook his head. *I can't get away even for a moment.*

Matt stood on the other side of Roz. He turned to watch one kit as it plopped onto a patch of grass. Matt tried again. "What's the matter?"

"Arthur signed me up for yoga." *Why am I so pissed off about this? It's just once a week.*

"Like he just signed you up to ref my hockey games when I first moved in with you guys?"

"Exactly," Lane said.

"And you found out about Daniel and Christine?"

"You knew that too?" *What else is going on that I don't know about?*

"Yep. Here comes the mom." Matt pointed at the gaunt mother fox. She had something in her mouth. She trotted effortlessly along the ledge. She dropped something in front of the kit who had gotten to its feet. The kit went to work devouring its meal. "What is that?"

"Probably a mouse or a vole. She looks worse than last time." Lane felt Roz's tense wariness through the leash.

"It won't be long before the kits will have to be looking after themselves. They have to have pretty amazing survival skills." Matt knelt and rubbed the fur on Roz's neck. "How's my girl?"

Lane smiled at Matt. Then he watched the mother fox. She turned, licked her lips, yawned and headed back to the full-time job of feeding her family.

"Can we hurry back? Fergus is coming to pick me up." Matt turned and Roz followed behind, forcing Lane to do the same.

✕

"This car smells great," Matt said. "Has anybody sat in the passenger seat yet?"

Fergus sat behind the wheel. He wore his red hair in a

Highland fro that made his head appear to be twice as big as it actually was. His freckles were more pronounced in the summer. He still weighed less than he should have at six-two. Fergus said, "My dad picked it up this morning. He took me for a ride this afternoon." The light turned green, and he touched the accelerator. "Five hundred horsepower!"

Matt was shoved deeper into the cashmere beige leather seat. "Whoa!" His right hand gripped the Mercedes-Benz armrest.

Fergus backed off the accelerator. "I want to see how it drifts." He turned left into a shopping mall parking lot.

Matt felt himself being gripped by the three-point safety harness. "This thing handles great."

Fergus slowed to ease over the incline and onto the freshly paved parking lot. "I've been keeping my eyes open for a fresh patch of pavement. This place clears out at night."

Matt looked ahead. Streetlights illuminated the pavement with a soft glow. Shops lined three sides of the lot. "Have you ever drifted before?"

"Nope." Fergus accelerated.

"Doesn't this thing have all-wheel drive and stability control?" Matt asked.

They approached the far end of the lot. Fergus pulled the emergency brake, turned the wheel and stepped on the accelerator. The Mercedes surged forward and they skipped over a speed bump. There was a shower of sparks as the front suspension of the car bottomed out and scraped the pavement.

Fergus took his foot off of the accelerator and stomped on the brakes.

The car jumped the sidewalk before plowing though the glass front of the Hallmark card shop.

Matt took everything in as if it were happening in slow motion.

The airbags deployed.

For an instant, shattered glass was suspended in a spider's web of opaque silk.

The nose of the Mercedes hit a display of greeting cards, then stopped.

Debris pounded the roof and trunk. A display teetered and fell against the windshield on the driver's side of the car. A hole appeared in the glass.

The engine raced. Fergus turned it off.

"Help me out of here." Fergus brushed crumbs of safety glass from his fro. As he rubbed his hair with his palm, blood began to smear his hair and hands.

Matt released his seat belt and bent his neck forward, letting his head dangle. The airbag had knocked the wind out of him and smacked him in the balls. "Give me a second."

Fergus undid his seat belt, leaned into his door and shoved his shoulder against it. "My dad is gonna kill me."

Matt raised his head. "I thought you said your dad gave you the keys."

"Actually, he told me I could take my mom's car, not the Mercedes." Fergus pushed against his door. "It won't open."

"This car is only a day old." Matt sat back against the leather, thankful that the pain was no longer so insistently pounding through his brain and groin.

"Let me out." Fergus lifted his right leg over the console.

Matt opened his door and stepped out. As he stood up straight, the inside of the card shop was lit with flashing headlights and rotating red-and-blue lights. He stepped gingerly over the glass and outside to the sidewalk.

Twenty minutes later, Matt was sitting in the back of a police cruiser when Lane and Arthur arrived.

An officer, who began to point at the Mercedes, intercepted his uncles.

Matt heard Arthur say, "We need to see our nephew before we do anything else."

Matt opened the door and stepped out.

He heard an officer say, "Crashing into a Hallmark store with daddy's brand-new Mercedes. Everyone downtown will love this!"

Another voice said, "Hey, shut up. That's Detective Lane. You know, the guy who took Smoke down."

"Are you okay?" Lane asked Matt.

Matt heard the emotion behind the question. "I'm okay."

Arthur hugged his nephew. "We were so scared when we got the call."

Matt cringed as his uncle squeezed his body. It was beginning to ache where the seat belt had held him back. The airbag had hit him hard and the resultant bruising was beginning to reveal itself.

"He's hurting, Arthur." Lane put his hand on Matt's shoulder. "Why don't you go sit in the Jeep while we talk with the officer?"

Matt walked to the Jeep. He saw Christine and Dan sitting in the back seat with the windows open. He opened the door.

Christine said, "Uncle Lane said *we* had to stay here."

Matt heard accusation in her voice. "How did this get to be about you?"

"At least I'm not the one who embarrassed Uncle Lane in front of the police officers like you did."

Just let her get the last word in, Matt thought. *Besides, she's right.*

He sat in the front passenger seat in the silence, watching Lane and Arthur listen to the traffic officer.

"How's Fergus?" Dan asked.

"An ambulance took him to emergency. He needs some stitches." Matt leaned back against the headrest.

Lane and Arthur turned and walked toward the Jeep. Lane opened the driver's door. Arthur squeezed in next to Christine.

"What did they say?" Matt asked.

Lane put on his seat belt and started the Jeep. "Fergus's dad is deciding whether or not to charge the pair of you with auto theft."

Matt felt his intestines dropping somewhere south of his navel. *How will I ever make this right?*

chapter 4

"Sorry I couldn't see you right away." Harper sat down in a chair on one side of the knee-high coffee table in his corner office. He filled it up and appeared uncomfortable in the deputy chief's uniform. His hand dwarfed the paper cup as he picked up the coffee Lane and Keely had brought with them. After a sip, Harper said, "You still know how to find a great cup of coffee."

Lane asked, "When's the baby due?"

"Two months. Erinn can't wait for it to be over and Jessica is all excited. Glenn is moving out into his own place but not very far away. He's moving in with —" he glanced in Keely's direction "— a friend."

"It's not a problem," Keely said.

Lane smiled. "My new partner is gay friendly."

"Good." Harper looked out of a window and turned serious.

"We've got a line on Kev Moreau. We may be able to connect him to the disappearance and murder of Zander Rowe," Lane said.

Harper looked at each of them in turn. The phone rang. He ignored it.

A moment later there was a knock at the door. Harper's secretary opened the door and poked her head in. "It's the chief."

"Urgent?" Harper asked.

She flipped her black hair over her shoulder and shook her head. "No."

"I'll call him back." Harper took another sip of coffee.

Lane's cell rang. He flipped it open, read the number and said, "It's Fibre."

"Take it," Harper said.

Lane pressed the face of his phone. "Hello."

"Early indications are that we have a probable cause of death," Dr. Weaver said in his usual monotone.

"Is the body positively identified?" Lane asked.

"Yes, of course. It is definitely Zander Rowe. The dental records confirm it," Fibre said.

"And the cause of death?"

"There is a precise hole in the skull consistent with a bullet wound. We have recovered several metal fragments and are analyzing them now."

"Anything else?"

"There is a nick in one of the ribs. There may have been two gunshot wounds." Fibre hung up.

Lane looked at Keely and Harper then said, "It appears Zander was killed by a gunshot to the front of the head, and there is some evidence he was also shot in the chest."

"Execution style," Harper said.

Lane looked at Keely. She was watching the deputy chief.

"Zander's brother is still in jail?" Keely asked.

"I assume so," Lane said.

"Can you check that out?" Harper asked.

"How come you two are tiptoeing around this one?" Keely asked.

Lane looked at Harper.

Harper shrugged as if to say, *Your call*.

"Moreau is really well connected in the city. You—" Lane looked at Keely "—already know from your undercover work that he's a member of the old boys' network that used to drink Scotch with Chief Smoke. He's also connected with various business and church organizations. The alderman in Moreau's riding is in his pocket. We also believe he has one or two contacts within the police service. The style of killing — a bullet to the head and one to the chest or heart — fits a pattern established since high school. Moreau was a suspect in several drive-bys during his mid to late teens. Unfortunately, we could never connect him to the killings. We have to keep our investigation quiet and move carefully. If it is Moreau who was involved in the execution — and Keely, you and I believe that to be the case — then there are too many possibilities for leaks if we don't keep things on a need-to-know basis."

"The pair of you aren't usually this cryptic," Keely said.

"Take a look at this." Harper handed each of them a magazine. Lane took it and read the front cover of the *City Insider*. Moreau's face smiled back at them with his green eyes. The headline under the face said, *Person of the Year*. The first issue of the magazine promised to keep the reader informed about the movers and shakers in the city while providing a taste of the good life.

Lane and Keely began to read while Harper leaned back in his chair.

×

Meet Our Person of the Year!

A different kind of developer has come to the fore and his name is Kev Moreau. From humble beginnings, this home-grown maverick is helping to revitalize his old neighbourhood. It is now a thriving community on the city's west side.

I met this twenty-nine-year-old at his downtown restaurant, aptly named Kev's. If you haven't seen the restaurant yet, it's hard to miss. Walls of glass, Italian marble, unforgettable decor and remarkable food.

We sit at a table next to the window overlooking the Stephen Avenue Mall, where we are able to watch the comings and goings at the Centre for the Performing Arts. After tasting the food, I'd say that art is also being performed in Mr. Moreau's kitchen.

Kev's clothes are tailored to fit him and those startling green eyes study me from behind a glass of red wine.

Yes — in case you're wondering — the wine is superb.

I ask him what he thinks of being *City Insider*'s choice for Person of the Year.

He studies the people on the street through the one-way glass before he answers. "To me it's an affirmation. I've grown up the hard way and to gain this kind of recognition is very satisfying."

I ask him about any new revitalization plans for the community he grew up in and where he continues to choose to live. Before he can answer, a very efficient waiter refills our wineglasses.

"I feel it's important for entrepreneurs to give back to the community. A variety of types of business development is what I like to see. It's locally developed, locally owned, and meets the needs of the people who live and work in the neighbourhood." Kev takes a sip of wine, then nods at the waiter, who promptly retires to the kitchen.

"Along with the economic prosperity, there has been a decrease in crime — especially drug-related crime — in my neighbourhood. I think this is my biggest accomplishment because it was done without the support of the police. It was an idea I promoted within the community."

I asked Mr. Moreau what's next if business is thriving and drugs are off the streets of his community.

"There are a few surprises coming. I'll be making some announcements in the weeks and months to come."

Lane took a minute to study the photographs. Moreau posed in front of a wall of bottles stacked in his wine cellar. Another of him leaning against a gleaming Maserati.

Lane looked at the byline. "Who's Andrea Wiley?"

"Apparently she's engaged to Moreau," Harper said.

Keely flipped to the front of the magazine. "Sue Pike is the publisher. Any relation to Moreau's man Stan Pike?"

"His sister. Getting the picture?" Harper asked.

"Starting to." Keely tossed the magazine on the coffee table.

"For more than ten years we've been trying to charge Moreau with a series of unsolved crimes. Each time we run into a wall of silence from his community. Witnesses either disappear or refuse to talk. We're pretty sure he runs his own organized crime network and manages to keep the competition away from his turf." Harper lifted his cup and drained his coffee. "Moreau thinks he can leave his past behind and move on to bigger projects. The problem is that there is always a body count when Moreau makes a move."

Lane nodded.

Keely looked at her partner. "What aren't you telling me?"

Lane looked at her. "He's a sociopath."

"So there are no rules?" Keely asked.

"Kev Moreau makes the rules." Harper turned to Lane. "Is Matt okay?"

Lane nodded at Harper. "A little shaken up. How did you hear?"

"Whenever something like that happens — especially if it involves the family member of a police officer — I hear about it. Besides, Matt is Jessica's favourite person in the world. I have to keep an eye on her friends." He smiled, then turned to Keely. "Inspector MacWhirter of the RCMP has been asking me to call him. I think he wants to know when you will no longer be on loan to us."

"Can you keep him on hold at least until we finish this case?" Keely asked.

Harper nodded. "The two of you need to be careful. Moreau has a reputation on the street for being ruthless and cold blooded."

chapter 5

"Okay, what's happened?" Keely sat across from Lane at a narrow table in The Diner on Stephen Avenue Mall. The restaurant was about five times as long as it was wide at about three metres across. She stuffed a fried potato in her mouth. "These things are so good." She chased it with a gulp of coffee. "And this—" she said as she held up the cup, "—it's wonderful."

Lane sipped from his cup.

The waitress arrived with a carafe and topped up their coffees. "Everything okay?"

Lane nodded.

Keely smiled and popped another fried potato into her mouth.

The waitress left.

"Well?" Keely asked.

Lane shrugged.

"Christine's on the pill." Keely pointed her fork at Lane.

"Did Arthur call and tell you?"

Keely shook her head. "Nope. It's just that you've got the same look on your face as my father did when he found out Dylan and I had moved in together."

"How's that going?"

"It's not." Keely's eyes narrowed to reveal a mixture of anger and hurt.

"Maybe we'd better talk about the case."

"Or about Matt and the car accident?"

Lane frowned.

"Maybe it would be better if we talked about the case." Keely lifted her coffee cup.

"We don't know for sure why Zander Rowe was murdered, we don't know who did it — at least we can't prove it — and both parents are dead," Lane said.

"Both?"

"The mother two years after Zander and the father five years after that." Lane looked at the wall as if peering into the past.

"Murdered?"

Lane shook his head. "The mother died of breast cancer and the father drank himself to death."

"And the brother?"

"He talked with me only once, then refused to meet again. Wouldn't respond to any messages. I'd like to try again but it's probably a dead end."

"I'd like to stop in and see Lionel Birch. He's got lots more to tell us if we ask him the right questions." Keely drank the last of her coffee and tried to catch the eye of the waitress.

"Like what?" Lane wiped his mouth with a paper napkin.

"Like how much he was paid to do the job. And how well he knows Kev Moreau." Keely stretched her arms, stood up and put money on the table. She looked at her watch. "It's early. Let's give him a try right now."

Lane set his share of the meal money on the table and followed Keely outside to Stephen Avenue. The morning sun reflected off City Hall and the windows of other buildings. They walked east down the mall, turned south at the corner, walked up to the car and got in.

She drove them west, out of the downtown core along the south side of the river and past the hospitals on the hill.

When they pulled up next to Lionel Birch's house, it looked much the same as on the previous day. The Starbucks umbrella was neatly wrapped up, the gate was closed and so was the back door. His truck was parked along the east side of the house.

"Let's see if he has a clearer mind when he's just gotten out of bed." Keely got out of the car. "We might get more from him this way."

Lane got out on the other side. "Let's try the front door." Lane felt the hand of the sun on his shoulders as they approached the truck. The day held the promise of heat. A faint scent of grease and cigarettes rose as they walked by the Ford. They stepped onto the grass and around to the front door.

Lane looked inside the front room window. Lionel was on the living room floor. Sunlight lit his face. His eyes were open. There was a hole between his eyebrows. "Wait," Lane said.

Keely heard something in Lane's tone and reached for her Glock. "What?"

Lane saw that his weapon was in his hand. "We just back away, call for backup and then get in touch with Fibre."

Within fifteen minutes the house was cleared, Fibre had arrived, the roads were blocked and the media was setting up beyond the yellow tape.

Lane stood kitty-corner from Lionel's house watching the arrivals. He turned his focus to the windows and curtains of the neighbours' houses. One bungalow was painted pale yellow; the garden was green and weeded, and the grass was perfectly trimmed. A sprinkler slowly swiped its way over the lawn, then worked its way back. He could see the roof of a vehicle through the garage window.

"What do you see?" Keely asked.

"A curiosity." Lane checked for traffic and walked across the street.

"Are you going to let me in on this?" Keely asked.

"It might be nothing."

"Or?"

"Let's see whether anyone's home." He pointed at the yellow house as he walked up the sidewalk to the front door. All of the drapes were closed, as were every one of the windows.

The glass set in the front door was opaque.

Lane knocked and watched through the glass.

A shadow fell along the floor of what Lane assumed was the kitchen. The shadow shifted.

He knocked again. "Keep an eye on the back door." He reached to touch his pistol.

"Weapon out?"

Lane nodded. "Just look around the back corner of the house. Keep out of sight."

The shadow moved.

Lane knocked. He could hear footsteps. The shadow moved closer. The door opened.

The man had a triple chin that looked like turkey skin. He weighed maybe two hundred twenty pounds and came up to Lane's nose. What was left of his hair was white. He looked at Lane's right hand resting on the Glock. "No need for that," he said as he opened the door. "Besides, I didn't see nuthin'."

Oh yes you did. Lane stepped inside the hallway. The house smelled of fried food and percolated coffee.

The man crossed his arms. "I live alone."

Lane reached into his pocket, pulled out his cell phone and dialed. "I'm in. Come to the front door."

"Who's that?" the man asked.

"My partner. She'll be here momentarily." He put his phone away and looked the man in the eye. "Detective Lane."

The man shrugged.

Keely knocked on the front door.

"Let her in," the man said.

Lane opened the door for his partner. He turned to the man. "This is Detective Saliba. What's your name?"

"Walter."

"Last name?" Lane asked.

"Shane."

"We have some questions." Lane looked around. The inside

shone like the outside. *There's a curious lack of colour in here,* Lane thought.

"You can ask." Walter took a deep breath.

"You knew your neighbour, Mr. Birch?" Lane asked.

"Knew?" Walter leaned against the wall and wiped at the sweat on his forehead.

He's trying to look nonchalant, but he's sweating too much. "That's correct. Mr. Birch is dead."

"Nuthin' to do with me."

Lane decided to increase the volume of his voice. "I didn't say it had anything to do with you."

"Then what the hell *are* you sayin'?" Walter leaned away from the wall.

Keely said, "That you saw something, you're scared and you've closed up your house even on a hot day like today."

"No law against it," Walter said.

Lane saw a tightening around Walter's mouth. The lines in his forehead appeared to be a centimetre deep.

"I'm not afraid! Who the hell do you think you are?" Walter's blood pressure seemed to pump him up so that he gained at least three centimetres.

Lane thought, *Now whisper!* "The fact is we have two murders. One was a young boy. The second is Lionel Birch. We think that the two may be related. The longer this goes on, the more likely it is that more people will die. Your answers have convinced me that you're not telling me all you know. If we walk out the door right now, we'll be back. If we come back, people in the neighbourhood will notice and word will get out." *Give him time to chew that over.*

Walter breathed. There was a whistling from his lungs.

Good, keep breathing. It means you're thinking. "You see, if we walk out your front door and move on to the next house, then whoever is watching will think that we learned noth-ing from you. If we come back to you tomorrow and the day after that then it looks like you've got too much to say. The decision is up to you. The smart move is to tell us what you know now. Then we move on to the next house and come back only if you call for us." Lane reached into his jacket pocket and pulled out a business card. He held it out in front of Walter's eyes.

Walter looked at the card, took it, pulled a pair of glasses out of his shirt pocket and read. He took his glasses off and stuffed the card into his shirt pocket. "I was watering the flowers in the backyard. Less evaporation in the morning so the plants can soak up the moisture, and it's quiet. I was behind the honeysuckle when this guy pulled up in a fancy car. He parked out front of my house. He had a couple of coffees in one of those trays. The guy went up to Lionel's house, went around the back and came out about twenty minutes later. He was whistling. As he walked he was working his hands. Then he put something round into one jacket pocket and a gun in the other. He was smiling. I saw him look around at the trees and flowers. He even closed his eyes like he was enjoyin' the moment. I remember that the birds were singin'. Then he got in his car and drove away." Walter looked at the door as if expecting someone else to come in.

Keely asked, "Did you recognize him?"

Walter looked away. "He looked familiar. Like I've seen him around somewhere." He lifted his glasses out of his shirt pocket and shrugged. "My eyes aren't so good."

"Could you identify him?" Keely asked.

"And you saw a gun?" Lane asked.

"It sure looked like a gun. It's just that . . . Well, the guy was so calm. So cool. Then you showed up and now it's a circus." Walter shook his head. "I don't want no trouble. It's summer. I just want . . ."

"You don't want to get shot," Keely said.

Walter glared at her. "Who would want that?"

"It's a thoroughly forgettable experience." Lane forced a smile.

Walter turned to him. "You've been shot?"

Lane turned his shoulders, pointed at his backside and said, "One of the most embarrassing events of my life."

"The pain?" Walter asked.

"Actually, it was what happened after I took the painkillers that caused the most embarrassment."

Walter chuckled and shook his head. "The problem is I can't be sure. I've seen the guy around but I can't be sure."

"Can you give us a name?" Keely asked.

Walter shook his head and tapped his head. "My memory isn't so good. It might come back and it might not."

"Will you call if it does?" Lane asked.

Walter took a breath. "Yes."

"Any specifics you can give, like the time?" Keely asked.

"Five-thirteen. It was five-thirteen."

"How can you be so certain?" Keely asked.

"I always know what time it is." Walter pulled up his sleeve to reveal a watch with a dial that would make Mickey Mouse proud. Walter's face glowed with embarrassment. "I can read the numbers on this one."

As Lane and Keely walked to the next house, she said, "He knows who the shooter was."

"He does, and if the shooter is that well known around here, then we have a pretty good indication of who killed Lionel Birch." Lane walked up to the front door of the next house.

$$\times$$

"You're not going to have a Nanaimo bar?" Lane sat across from Keely at a coffee shop down by the Bow River in Park-dale. Across the street, cyclists and joggers roamed up and down the trails running along either side of the river. Lane wiped his mouth with a napkin after eating a bowl of soup and half a sandwich. The sandwich was thicker than most burgers.

She frowned at her salmon sandwich. "I can hardly finish this."

Lane nodded and looked at his empty cup of coffee.

Keely covered her mouth. "Yes, you should have another cup. After interviewing fifteen different households, you deserve it."

"It didn't take Walter long to pack up and leave."

"I wonder if we'll ever see him again."

"Probably not, if he saw who I think he saw."

"Dude! You are so full of sh—!"

Lane and Keely looked across the restaurant where three teens sat around a table near the window.

"Don't say it! We got kicked out last time, remember?" This boy was maybe fourteen and wore glasses and a ball cap with an Avro Arrow jet fighter on the crown.

"At least let me finish my coffee this time, Bryce." This sardonic remark came from the middle-sized one with black hair and freckles.

Bryce had sandy-coloured hair that hid most of his face. He was the largest of the three and his voice was the deepest. "Okay, sorry. It's just that you're so wrong, Sebi!"

Sebi, the dark-haired one—his voice was changing—asked, "What makes you so sure of yourself?"

"You agree with me, don't you, Alex?" Bryce asked the one with the ball cap and glasses.

Alex frowned. "You're both wrong!"

"No way!" Bryce said, then leaned back on his chair.

"*You're* both wrong!" Alex said.

Lane looked around. The entire coffee shop was tuning in to the conversation.

Sebi said, "There's no way we'll still be friends when we're in our forties. And who knows if we'll live that long?"

Bryce poked the index finger of his right hand in the air. "My dad's still friends with the guys he hung out with in high school. They're like ..." He brought his hands together and interlaced the fingers.

"That close!" Sebi pretended to shiver.

"Sebi, you're so sarcastic! One of these times you're gonna go too far and somebody will beat the shit out of you!" Alex looked sideways to see if anyone had heard. He turned red when he saw all eyes on him.

Bryce pointed at Alex and laughed.

Sebi shook his head and pointed at his friends. "When we're forty? Yeah, right!"

Lane lifted one eyebrow and chewed the inside of his cheek.

Keely said, "What?"

Lane stared at the three young men.

Alex said, "Speaking of forty, it's my mom's birthday tomorrow. She's all stressed out 'cause she's turning the big four zero. She doesn't want anyone to know."

"Forty's, like —" Bryce searched for the right word "— really *old*, man."

"Lane!" Keely said. The boys turned to look at her.

Lane focused on his partner. "What?"

"You've got that look."

"What look?" he asked.

"That look that means you just figured something out."

Lane nodded. "We have to find out who went to school with, umm —" he looked around the restaurant "— our suspect." He looked at his empty coffee cup. "We gotta go."

Four minutes later, Keely drove them west on Parkdale Boulevard. The remains of their sandwiches were in a paper bag at Lane's feet. "Well?" Keely changed lanes.

"We need to see who Moreau went to school with. He came from the same neighbourhood as Zander Rowe and Lionel Birch." Lane stared ahead as if trying to imagine how they would manoeuvre around the roadblocks they were certain to encounter.

"When are you going to tell me about what happened to Matt?" Keely asked.

"When are you going to talk to me more about what happened with Dylan?" Lane asked.

"Smartass." Keely focused on the road ahead.

chapter 6

"Now keep your jaw loose. Remember to breathe and hold the pose," said Tonya the yoga instructor. She was about thirty-five and had more curves than a foothills highway, with a voice brimming with compassion.

Lane's legs began to quiver. He could hear Arthur's laboured breathing. They were supposed to be doing a pose called cowboy surrender. Their legs were spread, their upper arms parallel to the floor and their forearms at right angles. He looked around the room in the basement of Karma House. Eight other cancer survivors created their own versions of cowboy. Arthur was one of two survivors who had managed to coax a partner to the yoga classes. He, Lane and one other man were outnumbered by six females.

"Okay, you've all worked hard enough, it's time to get ready for Shavasana," the instructor said and watched as her students lay down and tucked bolsters under their knees and blankets under their heads.

They all lay on their backs, eyes closed and hands limply at their sides. *We must look like we're dead,* Lane thought.

Tonya turned on gentle flute music, saying, "Remember the breath. Start the inhalation down by your pubic bone and bring it up all the way to your collarbone before exhaling."

Lane concentrated on his breathing. The heat of the room and the gentleness of the music nearly emptied his mind before haunting memories arrived on tiptoes. For a moment he saw himself buried in a shallow grave. His nose, eyes, lips and chin were just above the earth. He began to wonder if anyone would ever find him. Next, Lane thought of the body of an infant buried in a backyard garden. *I wonder whether it's still there?*

×

Russell Lowell watched the customers at Kev's. The south-facing window was open to the terrace and then to the noises of the street. He could see people staring through the glass as they walked by, hoping for a glimpse of celebrity.

With two movies being shot in the city, it's the best place in town to spot an international or local celebrity, he thought.

He watched six people at a round table next to the water-fall where the spotlights and the copper-coated wall turned a sheet of water into a dance as it rippled its way over the ridges and dimples in the metal. The water disappeared into a blown glass base set up off of the floor. The light from the water reflected on the guests whose eyes widened as the food arrived. Conversation died. Knives and forks were raised. Morsels greeted lips and tongues. Eyes closed with pleasure.

Russell smiled. *Mary's right. I live for moments like this. When people's faces are transformed by the food I've prepared.*

He sniffed at the sleeve of his shirt, wondering what spice Mary would find on his clothes and what part of the fabric Joshua — their ten-month-old son — would moisten with his milky drool.

Time to go home, he thought as he looked up at the wide-screen television. Immediately, he recognized the face of the eleven-year-old boy smiling optimistically from the past.

Guilt drove a locomotive through Russell's chest. *Zander.*

On the way home along the freeway, he accelerated to a hundred forty kilometres per hour. Flashing yellow lights warned of an obstruction at the side of the road. The lights reflected off the yellow skin of a lowboy trailer carrying an oversized Caterpillar on its back. The tracks of the Cat hung over the sides of the trailer.

Russell's right foot shoved the accelerator to the floor.

He turned the wheel and aimed for the rear of the trailer.

×

Mary brushed at the long strands of blond hair at the top of Joshua's head. She stuck one stubborn tuft down with a lick of spit. He momentarily opened his green eyes — eyes the colour of his father's — gave his thumb a quick suck and closed his eyes again.

The hair popped up again like a palm frond.

Her ears picked up the sound of a car door closing. She heard footsteps and waited in the shadows created by the outside light shining through the front window.

A key entered the lock. The door opened. The foyer light made her blink. She heard his footsteps on marble.

She watched Russell's grinning face appear around the corner. He said, "Sorry I'm late. Has he been asleep for long?"

Mary smiled and stood while holding their baby close. She walked closer to Russell, hugged him with Joshua in between and said, "You smell of coriander tonight."

Russell smiled and reached for the baby. He brushed his hand across his wife's breast as he took hold of his son.

She brushed back her red hair and smiled. "What happened to you?"

"Nothing. Busy day at work is all," Russell said.

"Really?"

×

Lane leaned against the railing at the top of the Ranchlands Arena seating. The Zamboni driver was making his final pass. The ice was perfect — a light shade of blue. The Zamboni braked and eased through the gate. The driver appeared seconds later to scoop away a miniature mountain range of slush. The gate doors closed.

A player stepped out of the dressing room, into the players' box and onto the ice. His skates cut fresh lines in the ice.

Lane felt he'd like to put on his skates and take a few turns around the rink. Instead, he watched and waited while more players made their way onto the ice.

Matt was one of the last. He wore his new red, white and sage goalie mask. Howling foxes ran around the top and back of the mask. The chin, face and sides were painted with the jaw, nose and ears of a fox.

So that's what your new mask looks like. Lane tucked his hands under his arms and waited for the game of shinny to begin.

He watched Matt move to the blue line and begin his stretches. Lane shivered as he thought of the eleven-year-old Zander feeling the cold metal gun barrel against his forehead. *At least he wouldn't feel the cold of the hole he was put in.* Lane zipped up his jacket and tucked his hands into his pockets.

His mind turned to the case. He rummaged through the details, the interviews, the memories being unearthed while thinking over the files he'd written more than a decade ago.

Lane shifted his focus when he heard a puck ping off a post. He saw Matt looking over his shoulder as the puck went into the mesh above the glass. The puck dropped back onto the ice.

The unearthing of Zander's body stirred more images from the silt of memory. Tight-lipped school children and the parents who had taught them not to talk to the cops. A mother and father in grief. Zander's brother, Robert Rowe, staring blankly back at Lane as he interviewed him in prison, saying, "You don't understand. Our neighbourhood was fuckin' written off by the rest of the city. Parents from up the hill didn't send their kids into the valley to go to our schools. The police patrolled the streets. It seemed to us they wanted to keep the fuckin' child molesters and drug dealers in our neighbourhood. You think I'm talking to you about what happened to Zander? No way. We deal with our own shit."

Lane heard someone yell. He looked to the ice where an opposing player broke clear of Matt's defencemen. The shooter wore a white jersey and black pants. He shifted the puck from one side of his stick to the other. Then he snapped a shot. There was a thump when the puck hit Matt's blocker and the puck ricocheted into the corner.

After the game, Lane helped Matt lift his equipment bag into the back of the Jeep. Matt held a black bag under his arm. The helmet bag protected the finish of Matt's prized possession.

"How did the new helmet work?" Lane asked.

"Great. It fits better than any mask I've had before." Matt smiled despite allowing ten goals.

"How come you kept the mask a secret?" Lane walked to the passenger door and opened it.

Matt opened the driver's door. "I wanted it to be a surprise."

Lane climbed in and put on his seat belt.

"I've had the idea for the mask for a long time. It took even longer to save up the money. And I've been away from the game for a while." Matt turned his intense expression on his uncle. "I can't explain it. I saw this guy's internet site, sent him some ideas and this is what he came up with." He reached back and set the mask on the back seat.

Lane closed his door. "How come a fox?"

Matt put the key in the ignition. "I don't know if I can explain that either. It's just—"

Lane waited.

"—that foxes are survivors."

Lane said, "Fergus's dad, Hamish, phoned me while I was waiting for you to come out of the locker room."

"And?"

"He said he's not going to charge you or Fergus with theft.

Hamish has been trying to get Fergus to think before he does something stupid. This is Hamish's chance to force Fergus to think about what he'd done and the mess he got himself into." Lane studied Matt's reaction.

Matt took a long breath. "I embarrassed you in front of those other cops." He stared through the windshield.

"I wasn't embarrassed. I was just glad no one was hurt."

"I know. But a couple of officers were laughing and they said..."

"They said what?" Lane asked.

"They said you were the guy who took the bomber down and that you were the guy who stood up to Chief Smoke. They even thought you got rid of Smoke somehow. Then they said it was funny the way you could handle those two but you couldn't handle your own kids."

Lane smiled.

"Why are you smiling?" Matt asked.

"My own kids. I like the sound of that." *Matt's already feeling bad enough about what happened. He doesn't need me to add to the load of guilt.*

"I didn't like the way they said it," Matt said. "I'm gonna make it up to you."

"I was thinking about what you'll do to make it up to yourself. Besides, once I learned to accept who I was, I found it mattered less and less what others said about me." Lane waited for Matt to start the Jeep.

chapter 7

"Come on, Jessica, Daddy's in the car waiting for us." Erinn stood at the closet next to Lane and Arthur's front door. Her cheeks were flushed red. She blew air out the side of her mouth to move a strand of red hair from her face. "Arthur, the meal was wonderful as always. Thank you."

Arthur smiled. "Our pleasure."

Matt came up the stairs with Jessica. Erinn and Cam Harper's daughter was a clone of her mother. Same red hair. Same blue eyes. Same stubborn, independent personality. She had her arms wrapped around Matt's neck.

"Jess, time for us to go." Erinn smiled through clenched teeth.

"No!"

"Jessica Harper, don't start!" her mother warned.

Matt smiled at Erinn. "Jess, it's time for you to go home. You know you can call me on the phone any time you like. Come on, let's get your shoes on." Matt set the three-year-old on a dining-room chair.

Erinn handed him the shoes.

Matt bent to put Jessica's shoes on.

"I don't know how you do it, Matt. She won't do a thing I ask." Erinn shoved her fists onto her hips.

Matt helped Jessica to her feet, holding her hand. The heels of her shoes flashed red. "Jess, you can call me later before you go to bed." Matt picked her up and handed her to Erinn.

Jessica wrapped her arms around her mother's neck.

Erinn mouthed *Thank you* and backed out the door.

When the door closed, Arthur patted Lane on the shoulder. "I need a nap."

"We'll take care of the dishes." Lane picked up the plates from the dining-room table and carried them into the kitchen.

"What's the matter with Arthur?" Christine asked as she opened the dishwasher door.

Lane handed her a supper dish. "What do you mean?"

"Usually he relaxes after dinner. Has an aperitif or a coffee. Tonight, he just went up to his room." She held her hand out for the next dish.

"He gets tired. The operation took a lot out of him, and he needs his rest. Yesterday's yoga class really did him in." Lane reached for dirty glasses and cups.

"That's not it."

Matt brought the last of the dishes from the dining-room table. "She's right, that's not it."

"What is it, then?" Lane asked.

Roz scratched at the back door. Daniel opened it and held the dog by her collar while he wiped her paws. "Arthur's scared."

"Of what?" Lane asked.

Christine frowned at Lane and rolled her eyes. "Of getting cancer again."

chapter 8

Robert Rowe walked south along a barbwire fence line. He turned his brown eyes east when he heard a train whistle. The locomotive thundered and the trailing cars rattled along the track. He reached into the shirt pocket of the khaki-coloured canvas shirt he'd stolen from a clothesline in Olds, the first town south of the Bowden Correctional Institution. He'd escaped from prison the day before. He pulled out a carrot he'd liberated from the garden in the same backyard as the shirt. The shirt was a little large for his five-foot-ten, one-hundred-seventy-pound frame, but he figured it was better than too small.

He looked down at the jeans and black leather jacket that were a better fit. He'd pulled them out from behind the seat of a pickup truck. The unlocked truck had been parked near a hotel bar in Olds. He wore a black D&M Align and Brake ball cap he'd found out behind a tire shop. Robert figured he could blend in with anyone he'd be likely to bump into on the way south.

He pulled a magazine article from his other shirt pocket. It showed Kev Moreau at his downtown restaurant in Calgary. *I'll stay away from the roads,* Robert thought, *keep the railway on my left and make it to Kev's Calgary restaurant in four or five days.*

×

Lori stood at the open door to Lane and Keely's office as she said, "The secretary at that high school called back and she has three yearbooks for you. She doesn't remember

Kev Moreau, but she's going to ask around to find out who might be able to talk with you. She told me it might be difficult because only one of the teachers has dropped by to get things ready for the fall." She crossed her arms, then crossed one ankle over the other and leaned against the door jam.

Lane stood up from behind his computer and reached for his jacket.

Keely grabbed for her cup. "Guess that means we're on the move."

Lori flipped her blonde hair. "Did you notice?"

Lane looked at her pink jacket, white blouse, floral skirt and red pumps. "You look great."

"Love the shoes," Keely said.

"For a pair of trained observers, you two leave a lot to be desired." Lori turned her back on them as she walked to her desk.

"The new hairstyle suits you," Lane said through the door and followed Lori, who was nearing her desk.

Lori turned. "Too late." She smiled, sat down at her computer and laughed as they trooped past her.

Five minutes later, Lane held Keely's coffee as she did up her seat belt. She grabbed her keys and started the engine. Once they were rolling west along Sixth Avenue, she reached for her coffee.

Lane looked out the window at people walking along the sidewalk. A mother pushed a stroller. A senior sat on a concrete wall. A teen on a skateboard weaved around pedestrians while she swayed to music from her earbuds.

"You're quiet this morning," Keely said.

"This investigation could get very messy."

"Could you be a little more specific?" Keely guided the car under the Fourteenth Street Bridge.

"Zander Rowe is dead. Birch is dead. Once we get closer

to the killer, the violence could get even worse." Lane looked out across the river.

Keely accelerated. "You offering me an out?" She tucked the empty coffee cup between her seat and the console.

"You really should consider it."

"What about you?"

Lane shrugged. "I'm in. Once I get the smell of death in my nostrils, there's no turning back."

Now is not the time to tell him, she thought.

Fifteen minutes of silence passed before they reached the high school nestled in the valley of the Bow River. Keely parked in front of the main doors.

Lane followed Keely inside to the mezzanine where they turned right. A pair of janitors turned to watch as the detectives opened the door to the office and stepped inside.

A secretary had her back to them as they walked in. She turned and spotted the detectives. "I'm the only one in the office today. What can I do for you?"

Lane said, "We're from Calgary Police Services."

"You're here for the yearbooks, right?" She pointed at an overlarge manila envelope sitting on the counter.

"Yes, please." Lane took the envelope. "Anyone we could talk with if we have any questions?"

"I asked around." The secretary pointed a manicured nail at a name and phone number written on the envelope. "She taught English here for many years. She might be able to answer some of them."

Lane dialed the teacher's phone number after they got inside the Chev.

"Yep," a woman said.

"Roberta King?" Lane asked.

"That's right."

"Detective Lane. I'd like to talk with you about some of your former students."

"Which ones?"

"Kev Moreau and Lionel Birch," Lane said.

"Birch is dead."

"Yes," Lane said, "I know."

"When do you want to meet?" she asked.

Lane decided to adopt her abrupt style. "Now."

"I live just down the hill from the Foothills Medical Centre. Can you be here in ten minutes?" Roberta's voice had the raspy sound of bourbon and tobacco.

"Yes."

"Good, I'll put the coffee on." She gave Lane the address and hung up.

Eight minutes later, Keely and Lane stood on Roberta's doorstep. It was a two-storey house set into the hillside sloping down from the Foothills Medical Centre to the river. They knocked on a varnished wooden door decorated with hand-carved leaves.

The door swung open.

A black, white and tan dog greeted them. It appeared to weigh more than one hundred pounds. One ear stood straight up and the other flopped like a combover.

"Come in. Wally won't bother you." Roberta stood behind Wally, facing them. She was silver haired, somewhere between sixty and eighty, and stood at least as tall as Lane's six feet. Roberta turned around and walked toward the kitchen. Her clothes fit loosely and a belt held up her white slacks. "Close the door behind you."

They followed her inside. Lane heard Keely close the door.

Wally led the way into the kitchen where Roberta was pouring coffee into three cups. Sunlight poured into the kitchen through French doors that looked across the river valley.

"Quite the view," Keely said.

Roberta sat at the head of the table and sipped her black

coffee. She pushed at her hair. Wally flopped down with a sigh. "We're interrupting his walk."

In other words, let's get down to business, Lane thought before he asked, "What can you tell us about Kev Moreau, Lionel Birch and any of the other members of Moreau's social group?" He picked a coffee, added cream and sugar, and stirred. Keely poured milk and spooned sugar into her own cup.

Roberta looked through the detectives and into the past before saying, "Moreau was a real charmer. Good-looking kid. Even I was fooled by him for a time. Caught him cheating on a paper once. He smiled at me. Polite as anything, he asked if he could rewrite the paper, even if it wasn't for marks, and then he left. After school I went out to my car and all four tires were flat."

"Moreau did it?" Keely asked.

Roberta nodded. "Couldn't prove it, but it was him. It was a pattern repeated several times over a couple of years. One of the girls disagreed with him in one of my classes. She had a car."

"Four flat tires?" Keely asked.

"Yep. A few of the kids also told me that he was behind the drug sales in the school. Had the market cornered. He never got caught but it was common knowledge." She glanced at the dog, who harrumphed with his chin on the floor. "Don't you worry. You'll get your walk, Wally."

"Do you have any recollection of the time when Zander Rowe disappeared?" Lane asked.

Roberta focused on him. "Moreau was in on that?"

"We're looking into all possibilities," Lane said.

She smiled. "It's more than a possibility or you wouldn't be here. Just like it was more than a possibility that he supplied the drugs, cut my tires and burned down my garage."

"He burned down your garage?" Keely asked.

Roberta looked at each of them in turn. "I caught him cheating a second time. The garage burned the next day with my car inside." Roberta looked through the French doors at the river valley. "Again, I couldn't prove anything, but he let me know it was him."

"How?" Keely asked.

"He'd look at you a certain way. Smile at you a certain way. You just knew."

"Do you remember any other people besides Lionel Birch who were close to Moreau?" Keely asked.

"There weren't many who didn't try to get along with Moreau. The kids knew, the teachers knew that if you crossed him it would cost you. His buddy was Stan Pike. One of those lost kids who latch onto someone like Moreau," Roberta said.

"After we take a look at the yearbooks, could we come back and ask a few more questions if we need to?" Lane put his business card on the table.

"Better hurry up if you've got more questions to ask. I've got cancer. Terminal. The doctor gave me six months. That was three months ago." Roberta stood up, followed by Wally. "The worst part isn't losing your hair. It's this damned wig. It's hot and itchy." She took the wig off, revealed a smooth scalp and donned a black ball cap.

After Lane and Keely got back in the Chev, Keely asked, "What was that all about? The whole cancer thing was kind of odd. She was so casual about it."

Lane watched Wally pull Roberta down the hill. "I think she was telling us that Moreau can't get to her anymore. That the cancer has freed her of her fear of him. Or she doesn't care what anyone thinks anymore and just says whatever is on her mind."

Keely started the engine. "You really think that she's telling us she's no longer afraid?"

"It's the most likely conclusion. Cancer changes the way you look at life."

"There is another possibility, you know," Keely said.

Lane put on his seat belt. "What's that?"

"She called Moreau on cheating again after he cut her tires. She must have known he would retaliate."

Lane studied his partner. "That's true."

"Maybe she doesn't like people who mess with her. And maybe Moreau is a bit of unfinished business as far as Roberta is concerned."

Lane nodded. "You may have a point. People often have more than one motive. Let's get back and check out some of the names and faces in the yearbooks. Then we can ask her about any unfinished business."

✕

"I thought you had the day off," Mary said to Russell as she sat next to Joshua in their kitchen. Their son was wearing most of his rice cereal. She used the spoon to take some of the white from his lips, chin and nose. He reached for the bowl. She pulled it out of his reach.

"Pike called and said we're short staffed." Russell pulled on his jacket, then put his hand on Mary's shoulder.

"Pike doesn't make a move without checking with Kev first." Mary shook her head.

"Kev bought this house for us." Russell caressed Joshua's head and turned to leave.

"And you worked for it. It was supposed to be a reward for your hard work and talent."

"So?" Russell pulled his hand away from his son.

"How come we have no mortgage but you keep having to pay Kev back?"

"He's my boss."

"It's more than that and you know it." Mary went back to

feeding her son. "Kev may own you, but he doesn't own me."

"What is that supposed to mean?"

"He owns you. He uses you. He thinks you're bought and paid for." Mary looked in Russell's direction, but he wouldn't meet her eyes.

"You're being ridiculous." Russell's back was stiff with rage as he walked toward the garage door.

Mary shook her head. "You're forgetting what you say in your dreams."

Russell stopped but didn't turn, opened the door to the garage and said, "I haven't forgotten."

The door closed behind him.

"Kev Moreau won't own my son," Mary said. Joshua waved his arms, stuck his lips together and blew. A gob of pabulum landed on the right breast of her T-shirt.

She thought about the day Kev had picked them up and drove them to this house. Moreau was all smiles, saying things like, "It's about time you had a place of your own. The restaurants are doing well because Russell is such a talented chef. I've designed this house with the two of you in mind."

Then there were the eyes of the contractor when Kev pulled out a thick envelope of cash and told everyone within earshot how he was rewarding the loyalty of a long-time employee and talented chef.

Mary remembered how she felt obliged to smile even though she realized — at that moment — she was being bought along with the house.

×

Calgary Builder Wins Two Awards

Moreau Homes won two awards at the annual Calgary Home Builders' Association gala yesterday evening. Kev Moreau, CEO of Moreau Homes and local restaurant owner, was there to bask in the spotlight that shone on him instead of more established builders.

What's a successful restaurateur doing designing and building houses? That's the question any buyer might ask when looking for a home built by Moreau.

The answer will be found at the three Morningside show homes in the city's southwest. "We're relatively new to the game. We design homes that are meant to stand out. Homes that people want to own. In particular, we are targeting home owners who want something a bit out of the ordinary without paying a premium price," Moreau explained after accepting the awards for Best New Design and for Initial Quality.

Kev Moreau stands out in his tailor-made Italian suit and piercing green eyes. And his homes are as unique as he is. Moreau is integrally involved in every aspect of construction and design. He explains, "I was very involved. I was part of the process from conception to the completion of the finished product. Had I been afforded better educational opportunities, I might have been an architect or designer."

When asked about his future plans for development he says, "We're working on a few designs in the area of town where I grew up. It's part of a community revitalization project I've been involved in for the past few years. I've done quite well for myself and it's time for me to give back."

"See anyone you recognize?" Keely sat at her desk leafing through one of the yearbooks.

"Robert Rowe, brother of Zander Rowe." Lane held up the yearbook so that she could see a photo. "Here's Lionel Birch, Kev Moreau, Stan Pike."

"I'm going to start running names and see who's still alive." Keely reached for her mouse.

"There has to be some kind of connection here. Someone who knows what happened ten years ago." Lane stuck a sticky note next to Lionel Birch's face.

"But will anyone talk?" Keely stared at her screen and typed in the first name.

"There has to be someone willing to tell us what happened. Finding that person is the problem."

×

"Are you going to have any money left in a week?" Christine asked. She sat across from Matt and next to Daniel at the food court in the mall. She used a plastic fork to spear the last tomato in her Greek salad.

A toddler pushed his stroller past them. He was followed by the ordure of dirty diaper and his mother calling, "Come back here!"

Daniel—seemingly unaffected by the stink—demolished his second burger.

Matt pulled a cell phone out of his pocket. It was white and the latest model.

"Thin as a cracker," Daniel said between bites.

"What did you call Matt?" Christine's face turned red.

"The phone is nicknamed a 'cracker.' He's not calling me one." Matt gripped the phone between thumb and forefinger. "It's thin and fits almost anywhere."

"How much?" Christine asked.

"None of your business." Matt focused on his fries.

"You just bought that fancy goalie mask and now the new phone. Do you have anything left of your paycheque?" Christine asked.

"Since when did you become my accountant? I thought Uncle Arthur was the only one in the family." Matt glared at her.

"I just want to see you save some money." Christine looked to Daniel for support.

Daniel tried to talk, but his mouth was full.

"Since we're talking about putting money away, how much of each paycheque do you save?" Matt demanded.

Daniel choked.

"That's not the point." Christine patted her boyfriend on the back.

"God, you're annoying when you get like this," Matt said.

"Like what?" Christine looked at Daniel, who was red in the face and pointing at her. "What?"

Daniel wheezed. "You just told me you were broke, and you got paid last week."

"Shut up!" Christine smiled as she punched him in the arm.

Matt shook his head. "You're unbelievable."

"I'm not the one who thinks a new mask makes him an NHL goalie." Christine pretended to be looking for someone in the crowd.

Daniel shook his head, took a long breath and rolled his eyes.

Matt's face turned red. "You always have to get the last word in, don't you?"

Christine said, "You bet!"

Daniel stood up. "Will you two shut the fuck up?"

Christine's mouth dropped open.

Matt leaned back in his seat.

Daniel rolled the burger wrappers up in a ball, stood up

and pointed at Matt. "You did spend a lot of money on the phone and mask." Then he pointed at Christine. "And you blew your paycheque. Get over it!"

×

Robert Rowe was south of Didsbury and estimated he was about forty kilometres north of Calgary when he found the garden.

It was half an acre of potatoes, peas, cucumbers, carrots and raspberries. The garden was next to seven round galvanized steel granaries and a long-necked grain auger.

He gathered a few potatoes, carrots and peas, and then sat on shady side of a granary. After rubbing the vegetables clean on the thighs of his jeans, he bit into a carrot and felt his dry mouth fill with juice. Then he took his time shelling the peas and popping them into his mouth.

"Don't worry, Zander, I haven't forgotten about you. I'm just taking a bit of a rest. I'll be on my way after I dig into those fresh raspberries. You loved raspberries. Remember?" Robert looked south.

×

Lane rubbed his eyes. Then he used the cool base of his beer glass to cool his eyelids. He sat on the deck, sipping suds and watching Roz as she chewed on a rawhide bone.

We have at least two hundred people from Moreau's high school to check out. How can we narrow down the list?

Roz lifted her head. Her ears pointed toward the neighbour's house.

Christine, Matt and Daniel are out for the afternoon. Arthur is having a nap. Enjoy the quiet. He closed his eyes.

"Excuse me," a woman's voice interrupted.

Lane opened his eyes. A petite woman stood on the other side of the chain-link fence running between their houses. She was wearing black high heels, black stockings, red panties, a red bra and strawberry-blonde hair.

Lane closed his eyes. *You picked the wrong guy to get dressed up for, sister.*

"Hi. I'm your new neighbour, and I've locked myself out of the house."

Lane looked at Roz. Instead of barking, the dog cocked her head sideways and looked at Lane.

The woman continued. "I just slipped out the back door to put the garbage out. I'm cooking a special dinner. It's our anniversary. We just moved into the house. The back door swung closed. We haven't had time to introduce ourselves, and I…"

Lane shook his head and remembered his manners. "I'll get you a housecoat."

"And a phone, please. I need to call my husband. He has a house key." She crossed her arms to cover her breasts.

Lane opened the back door, went inside to get a phone and returned, handing the phone through the fence to the woman.

She took the phone. "Thanks." She dialed, fluttered black eyelashes and glanced at Lane. "My name is Maria."

"Mine's Lane." Then he went inside and upstairs to rifle through the closet, where he looked for, and found, a white housecoat.

"Lane? Is there someone here?" Arthur rolled off of the bed and stood up.

"It's our new neighbour. She just needed to use the phone. It's okay." Lane went downstairs with the housecoat. He opened the back door.

"Yes, right now! I've got supper on the stove!" The woman used her thumb to end the conversation and then held the phone out to Lane.

Lane opened the gate, walked across to Maria's gate, handed her the housecoat and took the phone.

He turned and walked back to his deck. When he looked

back at her, she had the housecoat on and was looking up at her kitchen window. She looked at him. "Do you hear that?"

Lane heard the sound of an oven timer. "Yes."

"My husband won't be here for half an hour." She stared at the window as if expecting smoke to start billowing out of her kitchen. "This is a disaster."

Lane thought, *Don't get involved!*

She turned to him. "I'm sorry. I think I've embarrassed you. Thank you for the phone."

"Not necessarily." *Oh shit, here we go, getting involved in a neighbour's life. It always gets messy. Remember what happened last time? You ended up with your house burning down.*

"Pardon?"

"Not necessarily a disaster."

The woman lifted her eyebrows and stared back at him with a question on her lips.

"I'm a detective with the city police service. I know how to break into your house."

The woman pursed her lips, considering her options.

Lane waited.

She looked up at her window. She looked back at Lane. "How long?"

"Sorry?"

"How long will it take?"

Arthur stepped out the back door, approached the fence and said, "Hello, I'm Arthur." He held out his hand as if meeting a new neighbour in her housecoat happened every day.

"Maria." She moved to the open gate to shake Arthur's hand.

"Not long. I'll get a bar." Lane stepped inside, went down to the basement and returned a few minutes later with a metal crowbar. By then, Arthur and the woman sat across from one another at the deck table, sipping coffees. Arthur winked at Lane. "You should always offer a guest a drink."

Lane looked at the crowbar. "The back door will probably open easier because you didn't set the deadbolt."

The woman stood and offered her hand. The sleeve of the housecoat was rolled up to her elbow. "Thank you, Lane."

He shook her hand and noted that her fingernails were painted red. "You're welcome."

By the time that Lane was able to work Maria's back door open, the smoke detector was screaming. "It's open!"

He waited for Maria who said, "Come on in."

Lane and Arthur followed her through the family room and up the stairs to the kitchen.

She removed a smoking pot of burnt chocolate from the stove.

Lane and Arthur opened the windows.

"Shit! It's ruined. He loves chocolate-dipped strawberries."

Lane looked at her through the clearing smoke.

Arthur handed her a tissue. "What's in the oven?"

"Lasagna."

Lane opened another window.

"Is it okay?" Arthur asked.

Maria dabbed mascara from her cheeks and then opened the oven. "It looks fine."

"Lane, go to our house." Arthur dictated a list that included cream and chocolate.

Twenty-five minutes later, the candles were lit, the table was set, Maria had reapplied her makeup and the smoke had cleared. Fresh bread, chocolate-dipped strawberries and a bottle of red wine were strategically positioned at the table. Lane and Arthur were back in their kitchen.

Arthur asked, "What was she wearing under the house-coat?"

Lane told him.

Arthur began to laugh. In a neglected cubbyhole in Lane's mind, an idea germinated.

chapter 9

"Let's start with his women. That includes the women prior to his fiancée." Lane looked over to where Keely sat at her desk.

"You think a girlfriend will tell us anything?" Keely applied a fresh layer of lipstick.

"I'm thinking more about ex-girlfriends."

"It may be the best shot we've got right now. That and what we can learn from Roberta King." She turned her head and appraised her look in a handheld mirror.

"That's true. Have you got a hot date tonight?"

Keely did not make eye contact. Instead, she asked, "So, do we call Roberta King?"

"Maybe she'll meet us for coffee."

Lori knocked on their open door. "Have either of you been told that Robert Rowe has escaped from Bowden Institution?"

"Have you been here before?" Keely looked at the bike path and across the river. Cyclists, joggers and oversized strollers vied for position. Keely shifted in the green plastic lawn chair under the umbrella.

"No." Lane looked along the pathway to see whether Roberta was approaching.

"That's a first."

"What's that?"

She held up her coffee. "The coffee's good and you've never been here before."

Lane smiled.

"Hello there," Roberta said.

Lane and Keely turned as Roberta — in her red ball cap, blue T-shirt and sweatpants — appeared around the side of the building. Her dog walked next to her. She sat down across from them at the table. Roberta handed the leash to Lane. "Can you hold him while I get a coffee and some water for the beast?"

"Sure." Lane took the leash.

The dog cocked his head to one side to inspect the detective. "Roberta looks even thinner than the other day," Keely said.

Lane nodded.

"What's his name again?" Keely pointed at the dog.

"Wally," Roberta said as she returned with a coffee and a bowl of water. She took the leash and set the bowl down in front of the dog. "I got Piked after you left the other day." Roberta's voice was almost cheerful.

"Piked?" Keely looked at Lane.

"Stan Pike's mother lives up the street from me. You must know that Pike is Moreau's right-hand man." Roberta took a sip of coffee, lit a cigarette and looked out across the river.

"What about Pike?" Lane asked.

Keely pulled out her smartphone.

"Pike and Moreau were thick as thieves." Roberta frowned and turned up her nose. "An accurate cliché, unfortunately. Moreau got his first shiny new car in grade twelve. Pike got one a week later. When they were in their early twenties, they bought new houses for their mothers around the same time. A few years after that, Moreau bought an apartment building and kept the rents reasonable so single moms and working families could have a warm, safe place to live. Six months later, Pike did the same thing. They stopped selling drugs in this corner of the city and stopped anyone else from doing the same. Around here, there are plenty of people who depend on Moreau. They think he's some kind of saviour. And in a way, Moreau's supporters do have a point. Many of the more affluent people in this city are content to look down their noses at this part of town. So Moreau's people keep their eyes and ears open. Most of them report to Pike whenever something interesting happens. This whole neighbourhood from here to the end of Bowness Park is Moreau's little empire. So when you to came to my house, someone told Pike's mother and she paid me a visit. Brought me some flowers because she'd heard I have cancer. But we both knew the visit was about my talking with you two. She said, 'I know you and Kev had your differences, but he's done a lot of good around here. There are plenty of people in the neighbourhood who depend on him. He looks out for them. They look out for him.' It was a warning for me not to talk with the pair of you."

"How come you still live in the neighbourhood?" Keely asked.

"It's my home," Roberta said.

"Did Moreau have a girlfriend in high school?" Lane asked.

Roberta studied Lane for a full thirty seconds before she said, "Yes, Candace Barnett, very attractive. She dropped out of grade twelve just before graduation. I never heard what happened to her after that."

There's something in her voice. Regret? Lane asked, "You know why she left, don't you?"

Roberta nodded. "Yes, I do. She told me in confidence. She worked so hard to graduate. I think her sister and her aunt know where Candace went, but they probably won't tell you. It's a very private matter." She looked directly at Lane. "The kind of thing a teacher still needs to keep confidential."

"What was the sister's name?" Keely asked.

Roberta looked across the river. "Diane."

"Last name?" he asked.

"Barnett. Do you two mind giving me and Wally a ride home?" Roberta stood up. Her eyes were sunk deep into their sockets. "I need a nap."

"Won't Pike's mother be upset?" Keely asked.

Roberta smirked. "Fuck her and the horse she rode in on. What's the worst Pike and Moreau can do to me?"

"How about the aunt's name?" Keely asked.

"Rita is the first name. Can't remember her last." Roberta jingled Wally's leash.

×

"I saw that puppet chick today," Matt said as he came upstairs into the kitchen. Lane was eating the supper Arthur had left warming in the oven for him.

Lane covered a mouthful of chicken breast with his hand. "What puppet chick?"

"You know the one — when we went to the rodeo — she put on that puppet show. No, they're called marionettes." Matt sat down across from Lane, picked up a chicken breast with his fingers and used his front teeth to rip it in half.

"You mean Aidan?" Lane speared a quartered tomato with his fork.

"That's her!" Matt popped the other half of the chicken into his mouth. He eyed the remaining chicken breast Arthur had left for Lane's meal.

"Go ahead and eat it."

Matt grabbed the breast before Lane could change his mind.

Roz harrumphed from where she sat under Lane's chair.

"Where did you see Aidan?" Lane leaned back and reached for his glass of beer.

Matt used his fingers to rip a strip of chicken off the breast. "I stopped at a coffee shop. She was in line ahead of me. She's putting together another show. She was telling me how her first show took her to New York, Toronto and Montreal."

"Wow."

"She told me a word in Cree. It's *mahkesîs.*" Matt chewed thoughtfully on a strip of chicken.

"What's that mean?"

"Fox. In the new show all of her marionettes are animals. I told her about the foxes living next to the golf course."

"She's very talented, and I admired the way she wouldn't give up when she got her teeth into something."

"Kind of like you." Matt popped the last morsel of chicken in his mouth. "Wanna take Roz for a walk and see if the foxes are about?"

Lane drained his beer. "Sure."

Fifteen minutes later, they approached the retaining wall near the golf course. They stopped on the far side of the road.

"Uncle Lane?"

Lane heard the anxiety in Matt's voice, stopped and waited.

Roz hit the end of her leash and growled.

"I still feel bad that I embarrassed you in front of the other officers." Matt let his head drop.

Lane said, "I've forgotten about it, so let it go."

A woman's voice interrupted them. "Oh my god! Waverly, come back! There are wild animals there!" Waverly was a bijou poodle with a shining black coat. Waverly had his nose down and his tail up and was running along a strip of grass above the first tier of sandstone. He advanced toward the fox family.

The mother fox appeared to be outweighed by at least fifty pounds. She called once and the kits disappeared into various gaps between the stacked stones.

Waverly barked and growled at the mother fox. The hair along the dog's spine stood up like tufts of prairie grass.

"Waverly! Come back here! They're wild animals!" She

looked at Lane and Matt. "Help! My dog is going to be killed!"

Lane checked for traffic and crossed the street. Matt and Roz followed.

The mother fox nimbly leapt up the sandstone wall and looked down from two metres above Waverly. The poodle attempted to climb the wall and managed to reach a metre and a half with his front paws stretched up the sandstone while his rear paws stayed on the grass.

One of the kits rushed out from its hiding place and bit Waverly's right flank. Waverly yelped. The kit disappeared back into an opening among the rocks. The mother fox bared her teeth. Her screeching bark made the humans shiver.

"Do something! They're killing Waverly! He's got papers!" The woman's eyes were open wide and magnified by a thick lenses set in designer frames. She was frozen in place.

Lane handed Roz's leash to Matt.

Lane hopped up over the first sandstone retaining wall and walked toward Waverly.

Another kit appeared, nipped the back of Waverly's leg, and then ducked back into a tiny cave.

Waverly yelped and his owner screamed. "Stop those killers!"

Lane grabbed Waverly by the collar and pulled him back from the wall. Lane then looked up at the mother fox, who yawned before disappearing from the edge of the rock wall.

Waverly growled, snapped and tried to bite Lane's hand. Lane dragged the dog over to his master. He stopped, looked at Waverly's tag and moved closer to the owner. She attached a leash to her dog's collar. "I'm gonna have the city exterminate those foxes! Waverly is a purebred!"

"Do that and I'll have animal control put Waverly down for biting me." Lane covered his right hand with his left.

"You'll what?" The woman began to back away.

"And I'll have you charged. Those foxes are endangered!"

The woman pulled Waverly along. "Asshole!"

"Back off!" Matt said.

"I got your phone number off the dog's collar!" Lane said.

They watched Waverly and his mistress step off the grass and onto the sidewalk. The owner's angry heels made an important announcement as she walked away.

"Is your hand okay?" Matt asked.

Lane held up a tattered sleeve. "Waverly got my shirt but she doesn't know that."

"Are those foxes endangered?"

"I don't know, but neither does she. I just made her believe what I wanted her to believe."

"I've never seen you bluff like that," Matt said and he smiled. "Those kits sure did a number on poor old Waverly. Just like you did with his owner."

×

"Lane?" Arthur asked.

Lane opened his eyes. His tongue felt like a beach towel.

Arthur, lit by soft shadows from the bedside light, had the phone in his hand. "It's Cam Harper." He handed the phone to Lane.

Lane closed his eyes, opened them and thought, *How come I didn't hear the phone ring?* "Cam?"

Harper said, "Sorry it's so late. Roberta King's house is burning. The fire department just arrived. Initial reports say the house burned from the outside in. I need you and Detective Saliba to meet me at the scene."

"Thirty minutes?" Lane asked.

"Thanks." Harper hung up.

"What is it?" Arthur asked.

"The woman we interviewed today. Her house is on fire." Lane pulled on pants and a shirt.

He phoned Keely before he left.

Lane pulled up to the scene. The flashing blue-and-red lights, the roar of engines pumping water and the heat of the fire on his face took him back to the night his own former home burned. He stepped outside of the Jeep and saw Keely waving him over. *How'd she get here so fast?* He saw that she had her nightie tucked into a pair of jeans and was wearing sandals. *She's back with Dylan.*

"I just got here." She pointed to one of the fire trucks. "Deputy Chief Harper is over there talking to one of the firefighters."

Lane sniffed and caught the stink of gasoline. "Any sign of Roberta or Wally?"

"None." Keely shook her head. Her eyes were black with rage when she said, "Roberta didn't deserve this."

Harper walked toward them. He shook their hands. "The captain says the house was fully engulfed when they arrived. The outside of the house went up first and there is a strong smell of a petroleum accelerant in the air. He's going to have to wait for the arson unit's investigative report, but he suspects someone created a perimeter of fuel around the house."

Lane looked at the houses near to the burning shell of Roberta's home. Roofs steamed while fire hoses wet them down. The nearest neighbours were sitting on a city bus as firefighters fought to stop the fire from spreading. All but one of the other houses on the street had its lights on. Most homes had faces in the windows. One bungalow had a light on in a back room. Lane walked toward the house.

"Where are you going?" Keely asked.

"I think we know who lives there." Lane pointed at the bungalow.

Keely and Harper followed.

Lane strode up the front walk, took the concrete stairs two

at a time, rang the bell and then pounded the door with his palm. He kept banging until the front light came on.

The front door opened. The woman wore a blue house-coat, curlers, blue slippers, three chins, makeup and an attitude.

Lane didn't smile. "I'm Detective Lane."

The woman shrugged and rolled her eyes.

"Did you see anything, Ms. Pike?" Lane asked.

"Not a thing." She shut the door in his face.

"A real sweetheart," Harper said.

"She's afraid," Keely said.

Lane and Harper stared at her.

"Isn't it obvious to you two?" Keely asked.

"No," Lane said.

"She's afraid of what her son did to Roberta King and could do to her," Keely said.

"How do you know that?" Harper asked.

"I just know, the same way Lane just knows when he's getting close to a killer," Keely said.

Harper turned to Lane and asked, "Why did you go after Pike's mother like that?"

"Just wanted to give Pike, Moreau and the gang the message that I'm knocking on their door. I'm coming after them." Lane turned back to Roberta King's house. Its roof collapsed and a shower of sparks burst into the sky.

Harper pointed at his chest. "Don't you mean *we're* coming after them?"

Mary woke up. Her leg ached. She opened her eyes to the soft green light of the alarm clock.

"Zander!" Russell's voice was oddly childlike as he lived the recurring nightmare.

Mary moved away from him in case he connected with

one of his flailing arms or legs. He was on his back, his legs and arms working the way Joshua's often did.

"It was Kev and Pike!"

Mary slipped out of the bed and turned on the light.

Russell's eyes were closed. His fingers were rolling up into fists. "They told me it was no big deal!"

Mary stood there, feeling familiar helplessness.

"I thought it would be okay!"

Mary heard Joshua crying.

"They said they wouldn't hurt you!"

Mary went to the door and opened it.

"They said you wouldn't be hurt!" Russell said.

Mary watched the sweat roll down her husband's face. Anger and self-loathing made her chest tight, and she felt the familiar heat of indigestion. *I should have made you move away when we were first married. We could have left the city. We would have been free of Moreau. Now you're tied to him.* Joshua's crying became more intense as she closed the door behind her. She left the light on. *Remember, you can walk away. You did it before. You left your parents before the booze could drink you up. To save Joshua, you might have to do it again.*

chapter 10

"Want to go to Matt's hockey game tonight?" Lane asked.

Arthur sniffed the air in their kitchen. "What is that?"

"It's me. I smell like smoke. Another person who might tell us more about Kev Moreau has conveniently died."

"So, what are you going to do?" Arthur poured himself a cup of coffee.

Lane thought, *Why not?* "I think it's time to pay Mr. Moreau a visit."

"You think that's wise?" Arthur poured a cup for Lane.

"You don't?" Lane accepted the cup and began to add cream and sugar.

"I don't. From what you've told me about Moreau, he's very consistent when it comes to dealing with threats." Arthur sat down at the table.

"You think I'm poking him with a stick?" Lane asked.

"Something like that. He's predictable and he's ruthless. And it seems he's willing to do whatever he needs to do to distance himself from the killing of Zander Rowe. Of course, the obvious conclusion is that Moreau killed the boy. And from the articles in the newspaper and that magazine, it's logical to conclude that Moreau has a rather sizable ego."

"And?" Lane asked.

"If you are able to link him to the killing of Zander Rowe, Moreau's freshly minted image will be destroyed. The city will forgive a reformed bad boy. It will not forgive someone who was involved in the execution of a child." Arthur lifted his cup to his lips.

"So I should leave him alone?" Lane felt his anger taking hold.

"I didn't say that. What I'm saying is that Moreau has been successful doing what he does for many years. To take him on, you need to be proactive." Arthur looked directly at his partner.

Lane opened his mouth and closed it again. *I hate it when he's right.* "The problem is that we don't have physical evidence or witness statements to tie him to the crimes."

"You're forgetting who Moreau is dealing with."

"What do you mean?"

"You and Keely won't give up. You've already proven that. Don't be surprised if Moreau is aware of your reputations." Arthur took another sip of coffee.

×

Lane and Keely walked single file along the wooden planks leading up to the front step of a nearly finished home. It was situated on a lot in an established neighbourhood close to the centre of town.

They reached the concrete stairs, and Lane stepped up. Keely followed, and they turned to take in the surrounding activity. A bricklayer was working his way around a pillar supporting an overhanging roof protecting the front entrance to the two-storey home. The red bricks reached about halfway up the pillar. At the curb, the finish of a metallic black Mercedes salon car glittered in the summer sun.

None of the men made eye contact with the detectives.

Lane turned toward the door.

"Lori figured we'd find him here." Keely stepped up to the door with its sandblasted glass. She opened the door, and Lane followed her inside.

The front foyer had tiled flooring and an open ceiling. The stairway had wrought-iron railings and allowed anyone going up the stairs to look down on the foyer.

Lane led the way into a combination kitchen and family room where Kev Moreau wore a grey golf shirt and black slacks. He was peeling bills from a wad of cash and placing them in the hand of a man who wore a white T-shirt and tan-coloured bib overalls. Both men turned when they saw Lane and Keely.

For an instant, Lane saw anger in Moreau's green eyes. Then Moreau smiled. "What can I do for the city's finest?"

Lane sensed Moreau's confidence, but there was underlying anger in the way he folded up the cash and slipped it back into his pocket. Lane said, "I'm Detective Lane and this is Detective Saliba."

Moreau looked at the workman. "I'll get back to you."

The workman nodded, went out the back door, stepped onto the deck and disappeared around the side of the house.

Moreau turned toward the detectives and opened his arms. "How do you like the house? I designed it from the ground up."

Lane looked at the nine-foot ceilings and the walls painted seafoam green. The floor was naturally finished birch, the kitchen appliances stainless steel and the countertop black granite. Everything fit together perfectly. "Very nice."

"We were wondering if you could tell us what you know about the disappearance of Zander Rowe," Keely asked.

"And the murder of Lionel Birch," Lane added.

"Did you hear about the death of your former English teacher, Roberta King?" Keely continued.

Moreau smiled. "Zander Rowe disappeared more than ten years ago. I went to high school with his brother and with Lionel Birch. Ms. King, yes, she was my English teacher in high school." He turned his back on them and looked out the windows along the north wall of the house. "What do you think of the way the light works in this room?" He turned and walked between the detectives.

Lane caught the scent of lavender.

"Come on up and I'll show you the rest." Moreau did not look behind him as he kicked off his loafers and climbed the stairs. He waited for Lane and Keely to do the same.

The steps were carpeted with thick nylon broadloom. Lane thought, *He could have done better than beige. Still, we'll play along, then hit him with another question.* He followed Moreau up to the top of the stairs where the entrepreneur waited and looked down on the foyer.

"The master bedroom has walk–in closets." Moreau led them into a spacious room with plenty of light and an attached bathroom with a Jacuzzi and separate shower.

Lane began again. "Zander Rowe's body was discovered in a building that was leased to your grandfather."

Moreau crossed his arms and stood with his feet shoulder width apart. "That's correct. The building used to belong to my grandfather, and yes, I worked for my grandfather for a year. I can assure you I had nothing to do with the tragedies that happened to these people. I think it's obvious I'm being very forthcoming with both of you. I'm hoping you will find whoever is responsible for these crimes." He looked directly at Lane.

But there has been a very subtle change in your tone of voice. You're saying the right words, you try to sound sincere, but I'm seeing none of it in your eyes. Lane asked, "How can we reach you when we have more questions?"

Moreau reached into his shirt pocket, pulled out a business card, handed it to Lane and said, "This one has my private number."

Lane took the card and handed Moreau one of his. "Just in case you have more to tell us. After all, Zander disappeared more than ten years ago. Memory can be a funny thing."

Moreau smiled and stuffed Lane's card in his shirt pocket. "You're right, of course." He shifted his concentration to

Keely. "Ms. Saliba and I are already acquainted. I hope you don't mind if I get back to work. I need to get down to the restaurant." His smile got wider. "Ever since I won the housing awards there has been enormous interest in my houses."

"The price is certainly right. How do you manage it?" Keely asked.

Moreau tapped his temple with the forefinger of his right hand. "Business sense and people skills." He stepped out of the bathroom, then out of the master bedroom and down the stairs.

"And cash," Lane said.

Moreau almost tripped but grabbed the railing and righted himself.

Lane saw a patch of red at the crown of Moreau's head where his hair was thinning.

In less than a minute, Lane and Keely were standing on the curb. The only evidence of their meeting with Moreau was the lingering scent of lavender mixed with the exhaust from his Mercedes.

Lane looked around at the workers, who were watching the detectives. Sensing Keely's anger, he said, "Hold onto it until we get to the car." After Keely closed her door and put the keys in the ignition, she said, "The bastard thinks he's untouchable."

"He may be right," Lane said. "If he's guilty, we have to tie him to the murder, and we've got nothing but dead witnesses."

"Don't you get it?" Keely started the engine.

"Get what?"

She put her seat belt on. "Every time we look for a connection between Moreau and the death of Zander Rowe, someone dies. Don't tell me you think it's just a coincidence!"

"No, but it does mean someone is very afraid of being connected to Zander's murder."

"Still, he thinks he's way too smart for us," Keely said.

"Then his arrogance is a weakness we can exploit. Did you see how he paid the workman in cash?"

"Yes." Keely shoulder-checked and turned on the Chev's turn indicator.

"The houses and the restaurants allow him to launder his cash. And he was a bit nervous when we walked in on the payment."

"So, you're saying the confident arrogance is a front?" Keely asked.

"That's right."

✕

Robert Rowe drank from a hose in the backyard of a house on the south side of Airdrie, a city just north of Calgary. It was the middle of the day and the neighbourhood was quiet. Most of the homeowners were at work in the bigger city. When Robert went to jail, Airdrie had been much smaller. Now he could see Calgary from here. He estimated that there were only two or three kilometres separating the two. "Almost there." He lifted his cap and ran the water over his head.

He lifted his eyes and wiped the water away from his face. He looked at the back step of the house. Someone had left a dandelion weeder on the second step. It had a forked metal tongue and a long wooden handle. Rowe dropped the hose and walked over to the step. He picked up the weeder. "This'll do the job."

✕

"How are things, Russ?" Moreau asked.

Russell Lowell looked up from the oak table at Kev's where he was finalizing an order of fresh fruits and vegetables. "Hello, Kev."

Kev Moreau still wore his grey golf shirt and black slacks.

He pulled out a chair, turned it around and sat with his elbows resting on the chair's back.

"Everything okay?" Russell felt fear gnawing a hole in his belly.

"Fine. Everything okay with you?" Kev smiled.

"Fine. Good." Russell looked over Kev's shoulder at the etched glass doors opening up to a grotto Kev had designed. He remembered Kev saying it reminded him of the one in the Playboy Mansion.

Kev leaned into Russell's line of sight. "Mary and the little guy doing well?"

"Fine. Just fine."

"I need to know that everything is good with you. This restaurant needs a top-notch chef and you're it. Patrons keep telling me you're the best in town. I like hearing that, and I need to keep on hearing that."

"Good to know." Russell waited for what he knew would come next.

Kev dismounted the chair, slapped Russell on the shoulder and said, "We gotta watch out for each other, you know. You and me, we're family."

Russell ducked his head. "You know it."

"I'd be real disappointed if I found out something was going on and you knew about it before I found out." Kev walked behind the bar and into the kitchen.

Russell felt his stomach heave. He just made it to the bathroom before he spewed breakfast and lunch into one of the Italian marble sinks.

×

Mary had her red hair tied back into a ponytail. She was throwing a load of wash into the machine when the doorbell rang.

She added detergent, closed the door and started the

machine. As she walked across the kitchen, her feet felt cool against the tile. She listened to hear whether Joshua was stirring from his nap.

Mary opened the door.

A smiling Stan Pike stood on the step. His close-cropped hair, grey golf shirt and black tailored slacks looked as if they'd just been pressed. His face was round and smiling. The smile caught her by surprise.

"What's the matter?" Mary looked over Pike's shoulder and saw his mother sitting in the passenger seat of his Mercedes.

"Mary." Pike touched her arm.

She caught the raw stink of gasoline and soap on him, and stepped back as his manicured fingers touched her flesh. The feeling of revulsion was overwhelming. *Every year you look more and more like a miniature Kev Moreau.* She tried to focus on his faux smile.

"We've decided to transfer Josh to a safer location." Pike smiled with his whitened teeth and opened his hands as if to show what he was doing was for the best and he held no weapons. He looked over his shoulder. "My mom will take good care of the baby. There's nothing for you to worry about."

Mary wrapped her arms around her ribs. "What's this about?"

"Just keeping everyone safe, nothing more." Stan kept smiling as he looked past her.

"I'll keep my son safe." Mary felt her hands forming fists.

"We've got more experience at this kind of thing. Kev wants me to take care of the situation." Stan let his hands fall to his sides. His smile was gone.

"Like you and Kev took good care of Zander Rowe?"

She saw his fist the instant before it broke her nose. The blow stunned her.

Mary heard Pike when he said, "Bitch!"

She felt her knees hit the marble floor. The toe of Pike's

shoe kicked her in the ribs, and she rolled up against the wall. For a minute, she couldn't catch her breath. She inhaled, coughed and spit blood. Mary heard Stan's shoes on tile and oak as he searched the main floor. Then she heard him as he ran up the stairs.

Breathe! she thought. Mary got onto her knees and hands. She saw the blood from her nose spattering the floor and thought, *I'll clean that up in a minute.* Mary stood up.

Move! She went into the kitchen. Mary swallowed the vomit at the back of her throat. *You've been hit before! You'll survive. Move now or you'll never see Joshua again!*

Mary was waiting at the bottom of the stairs when Pike appeared at the top with Joshua tucked under his arm like a football. Joshua looked at his mother. The baby's trembling lower lip and wide eyes told her he was about to cry.

"Move!" Pike said to Mary. This time he didn't smile.

Mary kept the kitchen knife hidden behind her right leg. She braced herself by putting her left foot in front of her right. She saw tears filling Joshua's eyes. A tear dribbled down his cheek and fell onto the carpet. His mouth opened and he howled.

"I guess you're a slow learner." Pike came down the stairs with Joshua held out at arm's length.

Joshua reached for his mother.

Pike's right foot reached the last step.

His left foot stepped onto the slate.

Mary glanced at Pike's leg. Her right hand swung the knife so it went under Joshua's feet. She felt the knife slow down as it cut into flesh. It stopped when the hilt and her fist hit Pike in the balls.

Mary looked up.

Pike's face blanched.

She released the knife handle.

Pike took a step forward. He looked down.

Mary reached for her son.

Pike released Joshua and reached for his leg. Mary took her son. *Not so strong now, Pike.*

Pike sat down on the bottom step and looked at her. "You bitch, you stabbed me. You know what that means, don't you?" He looked at the erect knife sticking out of the inside of his thigh. He looked at the blood on the carpet and the floor. Pike pulled the knife out. Blood spurted in an arc through the tear in his slacks. His eyes followed that first spurt of blood. His heart pumped. There was another spurt. Stan Pike stared dumbly, waiting for the next arc of blood.

Mary covered Joshua's eyes and walked to the phone. She dialed 911 and set the phone on its back.

She looked over her shoulder at Pike. He was slumped against the wall with his hand covering the wound. Blood soaked through his fingers, ran down his leg and along the instep of his shoe.

"An ambulance is on its way." Mary held her son closer, leaned over and put on her shoes. She walked into the kitchen, grabbed a baby bottle of milk from the fridge, picked up a handful of fresh diapers, stuffed the diapers and milk into a bag, grabbed Joshua's favourite blanket and walked out the back door. The stroller was on the deck. She put Joshua in the seat and strapped him in.

I need to call Russ and warn him. Mary eased the stroller down the steps and moved to the side of the house. She peered over the fence and around the corner. Pike's mother sat in the car, staring at the front door.

Joshua put one end of the nylon seat belt in his mouth.

Sirens sounded in the distance.

Ms. Pike looked over her shoulder.

The sirens moved closer.

Ms. Pike got out of the passenger door, walked around the front of the Mercedes and opened the driver's door.

The fire engine was the first to arrive. It pulled up behind Pike's black Mercedes.

The firefighter stepped out of the cab as the Mercedes drove away. Another firefighter pointed at the car. The others stopped to look as Pike's mother drove away.

Mary pushed the stroller down the driveway to the sidewalk. She turned left and walked away from her home.

A police cruiser approached with headlights and emergency lights flashing.

Mary knelt behind the stroller, reached for Joshua's diaper bag and hid her face behind the baby.

The cruiser passed her and blocked the road behind the fire engine.

Mary opened a package of baby wipes and used one to wipe the blood from her face and where the blood had spattered her feet and shins. Stars appeared in front of her eyes when she wiped the blood from her nose. She wiped her hands, stood up and walked down the street. An ambulance flashed past her twenty seconds later. The wind from its wake helped evaporate the moisture on her face. She checked her purse and realized that her phone was still in the kitchen. *Get Joshua away from here, then phone Russell,* she thought.

×

Russell placed a garnish of cilantro on shrimp flambéed in a butter, garlic and whiskey sauce. He cringed when four fingernails and a thumb dug painfully into the flesh between his shoulder and neck.

"We need to talk," Kev Moreau said.

Russell saw the black of Kev's pupils and felt a clenching just under his ribs as he turned to follow Moreau.

Moreau kept an office at the back of the kitchen. He opened the door for Russell and closed the door behind them.

"Sit down," Moreau growled. It was the sound a predator makes at the back of its throat when it is about to attack.

Russell sat in front of a desk made of polished Argentinean wood. Kev had bought the black mesquite desk in southern California and had it shipped north. *It took six of us to haul this desk from the truck into the office,* Russell thought. Kev sat behind the desk in a black leather chair, rubbing his hands over the polished wood surface.

Russell looked at the poster Kev had made of his cover on *City Insider* magazine. It was three times the size of the regular Kev. "We've got a bit of a situation. Pike and his mom went over to your place with a gift for the baby. His mom just called me. The police showed up at your house, so she had to leave without Pike."

Russell shook his head. "What are you talking about? Are Mary and Joshua okay?"

"Now I'm hearing is that Mary's not in the house, the baby is gone and Pike is dead." Kev leaned forward, his green eyes focused on Russell.

Russell looked to Moreau's right. He saw the cardboard filing boxes stacked in the corner. He remembered the day Moreau had called him into the office and reached into the top box. Moreau pulled out stacks of twenty- and fifty-dollar bills. Kev had set them on the desk, placed the money in two grocery bags and said, "This should cover the cost of furniture for the new house with a bit left over. I always take care of my people."

Russell looked at Moreau.

"Where would Mary go? To her mother's?" Kev asked.

"I don't think so. And she hasn't called me. I don't know where she is." Russell stared at the dark surface of the desk.

"You know that if you hear anything, I'm the first person you should talk to. Right?" Moreau tapped the top of the desk with the index finger of his right hand.

Russell nodded. "Right."

"Good. We need to count on one another. Just remember, I've got your back." Kev pushed his chair back and stood.

Russell also stood and walked out the door. He felt a drop of sweat running down his spine. He went back to the table to finish the order but couldn't focus on the paper. He kept wondering why Pike and his mom had gone to see Mary in the first place.

×

"You coming to my game tonight? It's an early one." Matt wasn't able to keep the expectation from his voice.

"Seven o'clock, right?" Lane asked. *Ever since you got that new phone, I hear from you at least twice a day.* He looked out the window of the Chev. Lane saw the dual wheels of a semi in the next lane.

"See you there." Matt hung up.

Lane's phone rang again immediately. He looked over at Keely, who accelerated along Glenmore Trail and across the causeway. On his left he could see the sails of boats scattered across the width and breadth of the reservoir.

He tapped the face of the phone with his thumb and put it to his ear. "Hello?"

"It's Harper."

"Oh, Cam, what's new?" Lane asked.

"I need you and Keely to head over to an address in the northwest. Stan Pike is the initial ID on the deceased. First reports indicate it's a homicide. The forensics unit is on its way." Harper gave Lane the address.

"How come you're calling me directly?" Lane asked, then looked at Keely. He pointed at an approaching interchange and indicated that she needed to turn right.

"Stan Pike's brother is on the force. I need to know as much as possible about Pike's death, and I need it right away. The information needs to come directly from someone I trust." Harper hung up.

Lane turned to Keely. "We need go to Nose Hill Drive. I'll direct you from there." Twenty minutes later, they pulled up in front of a two-storey house overlooking the river valley and the mountains. An ambulance and police cruisers were parked out front, blocking the driveway. Keely parked in front of a house at the neck of the cul-de-sac. She nodded in the direction of the house where the body was found. "Who owns the house?"

"Not sure yet," Lane said. They got out of the car and looked ahead at the home with an open front door. "If it's Pike who's dead, then the game has changed. Things could get even more vicious from here on in."

"I thought it was pretty vicious already." Keely walked beside him.

"Pike is Moreau's man. If Moreau was getting itchy when we started looking into Zander Rowe's disappearance, he'll be scratching now and his claws will come out. Moreau's a predator. His instinctual reaction is to eliminate threats. We have to be ready for almost anything." Lane gestured for Keely to go first as they passed the ambulance with its open back doors. A female staff sergeant with black braided hair approached them. "Stephens, this is Keely Saliba."

Staff Sergeant Kaye Stephens offered a hand to Keely. "Good to meet you, Detective."

"Likewise," Keely said.

Stephens nodded in the direction of the open front door. "It was open when the firefighters arrived. They could see he was dead: eyes open, pupils fixed and dilated. I took a look inside the door and could see who it was. So I told everybody else to back off until you could get here."

"The forensics unit is on its way. Mind if we take a peek?" Lane asked.

"Up to you. It looks like he was stabbed in the leg. My bet is it was a woman who got him."

"What makes you think that?" Keely asked.

"Pike was cut high up on the thigh. It's hard to tell for certain with all the blood, but it appears he was stabbed close to the balls. Looks like a woman's work to me." Stephens waited for a comeback from Keely.

Keely frowned. "Pike is — or was — Moreau's right-hand man, right?"

Lane moved closer to the front door while listening to the conversation.

Stephens said, "That's right."

"This is his house, then?"

Stephens shook her head. "It's owned by Mary and Russell Lowell."

"Who are they?"

"Not sure at this point."

"Anybody else in the house?" Keely asked.

"I checked for any other victims. I used the back entrance. That door was left open too. The house was empty except for Pike." Stephens looked sideways at Keely.

Lane stood on the sidewalk and looked inside the front door. The smell of blood sneaked outside. Pike was sitting on the bottom stair of a two-metre-wide staircase. His head leaned against the wall. His eyes stared at something to Lane's left. The blood pooled under Pike's bloody hands, as if he'd tried to stem the flow. A black-handled carving knife lay in the blood pool running from the steps to beyond Pike's extended left leg. His right shoe was filled with blood.

Keely stood next to Stephens. "What did you find when you went inside?"

"Baby's room upstairs. No baby. Coffee pot still on in the kitchen. Cell phone on the kitchen table. A load of wash just finished before you got here. The washer's buzzer scared the shit out of me when I walked past the laundry-room door. Nothing downstairs. No car in the garage. No baby stroller." Stephens looked at Lane as he turned around.

He said, "Look's like the knife severed the femoral artery. If the artery was cut at an angle, exsanguination might take two minutes."

"Exsanguination? Speak English, Detective," Stephens said.

Lane turned to face the staff sergeant. "We need to get confirmation from forensics but there is separate blood spatter on the floor. It's away from the main pool by Pike. If it's another blood type, then we have a better idea of what happened here."

The Forensic Crime Scene Unit van pulled up and parked in the driveway of the neighbour's house.

Dr. Colin Weaver looked in their direction, appeared not to see them and began to shimmy his way into a white bunny suit.

Stephens looked at Lane. "You and Weaver still have a problem after that racist remark he made to your niece?"

"Actually, things have been pretty good lately."

"Pretty good? The guy can't do enough for you. Fibre always takes real good care of his friend Detective Lane," Keely said.

"You're kidding, right?" Stephens asked.

"Not at all." Keely smiled.

Fibre approached with his eyes on the ground.

"Colin?" Lane asked.

Fibre raised his head. He had three days of stubble on his face. "The fire at the King home was deliberately set. An accelerant was used to surround the house. And, yes, Roberta King died in the fire. Dental records confirm it. Also, it looks like two shots killed Zander Rowe. One shot to the head and another to the heart." Fibre used his usual monotone before stepping between them and walking toward the house without a word of apology.

Lane caught the scent of body odour and unwashed clothes. *He's usually clean shaven and smelling of soap.* "When did you get the results?"

"Yesterday." Fibre stopped and set a plastic forensic tool kit on the step.

"How come you didn't phone me?"

Fibre turned to Lane. "I forgot."

"Really? That's not like you." Keely crossed her arms under her breasts.

Fibre looked at his feet. "Where's the body?"

"Just inside the door." Lane moved close and glanced to the right to direct Fibre toward the body.

"I need to talk to you —" Fibre lifted his eyes to look directly at Lane "— after."

Fifteen minutes later, Fibre's team arrived. They pulled on their bunny suits and walked silently up the steps and into the house.

"What did Fibre mean about wanting to talk with you?" Keely sipped coffee while she watched the forensics team work through the open front door.

"You know as much as I do." Lane sipped a black coffee and wondered where he could find some cream and sugar.

"So, what's next?" Keely asked.

"What do you mean?"

"This is murder number four if we include Roberta King. What do you think we need to do to get ahead of Kev Moreau?" Keely watched Lane from over top the rim of her coffee cup.

"This murder is different from the others. Pike was at the top of the Moreau hierarchy. None of the other killings were this close to Moreau." Lane watched Fibre come through the front door. Dr. Weaver stepped down the front stairs. At the sidewalk, he waved at Lane and pointed at the Chev.

"Talk to me." Fibre walked past them. Keely and Lane followed. Fibre waited for them to unlock the car before getting in the back and shutting the door. Lane got into the front seat on the passenger side. Keely got in behind the wheel and closed the door. Fibre pulled his white hood back then combed his hair with his fingers. "I'm in trouble." Lane looked at Keely, who made an almost imperceptible shrug of the shoulders.

"What kind of trouble?" Lane caught the intensely sour smell of Fibre's atypical lack of hygiene.

Fibre looked out the side window. "I'm going to be a father. The mother wants child support."

I would never have guessed that was what Fibre was about to say. "When is the child due?"

"Children. It's a multiple birth. The mother was on fertility drugs. We met at a convention in Seattle. She invited me to her hotel room. We had sex. Lots of sex." Dr. Weaver did not smile.

"How many children?" Keely asked.

"Three." Fibre stared out the side window again.

"What do you want to do?" Lane asked.

Fibre focused on Lane before he answered. "Be a father."

"Where does the mother live?" Keely asked.

"Here. In the city."

Keely looked at Lane.

"What kind of help can I give you?" Lane asked.

"She invited you up to her room?" Keely asked.

Fibre nodded.

"Where were you when that happened?" Keely asked.

"I was eating dinner in the hotel restaurant and she asked if she could join me. We finished dinner. Then we went for a walk." Fibre watched Keely more intently.

"She told you she was on fertility drugs?" Keely asked as she looked at Lane.

"Not until she phoned this week," Fibre said.

Lane frowned and asked Keely, "What are you saying?"

Keely looked at Fibre. "Had you met the woman before the convention?"

"At the university. Sometimes I'd see her at lectures or readings." Fibre frowned and looked from Lane to Keely. "Why are you asking me these questions?"

"Just a few more. She ever talk to you?" Keely asked.

Fibre nodded. "Sometimes."

"You ever talk with her?" Keely asked.

Fibre blushed. "I'm not very good at conversation."

"Is she married?" Keely asked.

"No."

"Then why was she on fertility drugs?" Keely raised her eyebrows. Fibre looked at Lane.

Keely said, "There is a very high probability that she planned to meet you at the convention and that she planned on getting pregnant."

"Planned?" Fibre asked.

"Yes, planned," Lane said.

"She was hot for you." Keely pointed at Fibre. "It's very probable that she wanted to get pregnant, and she made sure she found you at the convention."

"Why?" Fibre looked at Keely in stunned amazement.

"Dr. Weaver, you're apparently not aware of it, but you are a very attractive man," Keely said.

"I am?" Fibre leaned to look at his face in the rear-view mirror.

"Are you rich?" Keely asked.

Fibre's lips pursed and his eyebrows met as he considered the question.

"How much money do you have in the bank?" Keely asked.

Lane thought, *She's good with him. Blunt when she needs to be and gentle when need be.*

"Today?" Fibre asked.

"What do you mean?" Keely asked.

"How much money do I have today?" He frowned and appeared to do a mental calculation.

"How much money did you have yesterday?" she asked.

"My lawyer says I shouldn't divulge that information." Fibre crossed his arms and leaned back in his seat.

"You asked us for help," Keely said.

"Enough. That's all I'm going to say about my finances." Fibre closed his mouth tight.

Keely looked at Lane.

My turn! Lane said, "You have a lawyer, so make an appointment. Find out what the woman . . . What's her name?"

"Gaia. It means Earth Mother in some cultures."

Lane looked at Fibre to see whether he was going to continue, but Fibre closed his mouth again and looked out the window. "Ask your lawyer to find out what Gaia wants. When are the babies due?"

"In four months."

"Do you have a house?" Lane asked.

Fibre frowned.

"How many houses do you have?" Lane asked.

"Ummmm."

"Can you afford to buy a house big enough for three babies and a full-time nanny?" Lane asked.

Fibre considered the question.

Let him do the math. He's probably better at it than I am, Lane thought.

"Yes." Fibre looked out the window again.

"So you can afford to take care of the kids on your own if you need to. All you have to do is find out what this Gaia wants. Let your lawyer work it out for you. Just make it clear that you want to play a big part in the lives of your children." Lane tapped the back of his seat to get Fibre to look at him.

A frown lined Fibre's forehead as he turned to Lane. "That's all I have to do?"

Lane shrugged. "Well, yeah. That's all for now. Pretty soon you'll be a very busy man."

Fibre rubbed his nose. He closed his eyes and inhaled.

Now that that's taken care of, I bet he'll shift right back to the case, Lane thought.

Fibre wrinkled his nose. "I smell bad. About the deceased. His ID says that he is Stanley Pike. It appears the femoral artery was cut at an angle. He may have bled to death in less than two minutes. Also, I took scrapings from under his fingernails. There was the lingering odour of what might be gasoline on his hands and shoes."

"Do you think he set the fire at Roberta King's house?" Keely asked.

"I'm going to take samples from the accelerants used at the King fire and compare them with the residue on Pike's hands and shoes to see if they're similar. Also, I have his wristwatch. It smelled strongly of gasoline; the strap was saturated with it. We may have a link between the two crimes." Fibre reached to open the door.

"Where are you going?" Keely asked.

Fibre looked back at her. "To phone my lawyer." He opened his door. There was the scream of brakes and a horn blasted the inside of the Chev. Fibre closed his door. "Oh my goodness."

Keely looked over her shoulder as a man of about thirty climbed out of the car that had nearly hit the doctor.

"What happened?" Fibre asked.

Lane opened his door, got out, looked over the roof of the car and asked, "Is there a problem?"

The young man was as tall as Lane and wearing a chef's white jacket. He said, "That's my house!" He pointed at the open front door where Pike's body was being manoeuvred outside on a gurney. The body was covered with a red blanket.

"What is your name?" Lane asked.

"Mary? What happened to Mary?" the man asked as he stood paralyzed.

"The victim is a male." Lane watched the young man's eyes look right and left.

"Where's Mary? Where's Josh?" The man tried to walk around Lane.

Lane put his hand up. "What's your name?"

"Russell Lowell. I live in that house with Mary and Joshua." Russell attempted to push Lane's hand away.

Lane stepped in front of Russell. "There was only one person found in the house. The body is not your wife's or your son's. You can't go in there right now."

Russell shook his head. "Where are they?"

Lane watched Fibre get out of the back seat and walk to the FCSU van.

"We don't know that. All we do know is that a man bled to death at the bottom of the stairs, just inside your front door." Lane watched as Keely came around to the other side of Russell.

"Who is the dead man?" Russell asked.

Lane thought, *This might help us.* "Perhaps you could help us with identification. Are you willing?"

Keely opened her mouth to say something and stopped when Lane glared at her.

Russell looked at his house and the body being loaded into the back of an ordinary-looking red minivan parked beside the larger blue–and–white FCSU van. "Okay."

Lane walked on one side of Russell, Keely on the other. When they got to the van, Lane faced the driver. "We need to take a look at the victim."

The driver of the red minivan was about forty, wore a white shirt and jeans and played with the keys. "I'm supposed to deliver this one right away for an autopsy."

Lane ignored the driver and untucked the red blanket, revealing the face of the victim and his open-eyed stare.

Russell asked, "Was there a gift near Pike's body?"

"A what?" Lane asked.

Russell looked away from the corpse. "We used to joke because Pike had his own tanning bed so that he could look more like Moreau. But Moreau was almost a foot taller." He looked at Lane and continued. "I told Kev he had nothing to worry about, that I would keep my mouth shut. But Kev always needs to have insurance."

Listen to him carefully. Let him ramble if he wants, Lane thought.

Russell turned away from the body.

Lane and Keely followed him.

Lane heard the gurney sliding over the floor of the van. Then the rear door shut.

"Who has nothing to worry about?" Keely asked.

Russell looked at her. He shook his head. "No one."

"If we find Mary and Joshua safe, will you talk with us then?" Lane asked.

Russell shrugged and walked toward his house.

"Why did you ask if there was a gift by the body?" Lane called after Russell, who stood at the foot of the stairs and looked inside of his house.

Keely leaned close to Lane. "Sorry. I thought I could get him to talk."

"Don't be sorry." Lane's phone rang. He picked it out of his pocket. "Lane."

"Harper."

There's something wrong. It's in his voice.

"Lane, Jessica's missing," Harper said.

"What?" Lane asked.

"Erinn took her shopping. She thought Jessica was right behind her. We've turned the mall upside down. Jessica is gone."

"What happened?" Keely asked.

Lane held up his left hand.

"Find out if Arthur, Christine and Matt are all right," Harper said and hung up.

"What?" Keely asked.

Lane continued to hold up his left hand while he dialed with his right. "Arthur?"

"Are you going to be home for supper?" Arthur asked.

"Where are the kids?" Lane asked.

"Christine and Dan are downstairs watching TV. Matt's gone to his hockey game. Remember, he asked us to go. What's the matter?" Arthur asked.

Think!

"Lane?" Arthur asked.

"I'll call you back." Lane tapped the face of the phone with his thumb and looked at Keely. "We have to go." He dialed Matt's cell. It rang three times. The connection opened and closed. Lane dialed again. It rang five more times before a recorded voice said, "The customer you are calling is not available." Lane dialed the number of the dispatcher, then turned to Keely. "You drive."

"Calgary . . ." the dispatcher said.

"I need units at the Crowchild hockey arena," Lane said and gave her the address. Then he looked at Keely. "You need to call your family."

It was a fifteen-minute drive to the twin arenas. Keely got them there in ten. Three cruisers were already on the scene with their lights flashing. They blocked each of the exits to a brown-and-grey building near the crest of a hill.

Keely stopped at the front door and followed him. He pulled the arena door open and checked the arena assignments on the whiteboard. *Matt'll be in net and it'll all be okay.* He turned right, walked through a second set of doors and into the rink area. The cold, dry air enveloped him. A goalie was in net at this end. His helmet was a solid blood red. Lane stepped up into the stands so he could see the other net from above the distortion of the Plexiglas. The other net was empty. He ran to the second arena. The Zamboni was layering a fresh coat on the ice. Lane ran down the hallway, pushing and pounding each of the dressing room doors. Only two were opened. At the first, startled players looked up as he asked, "Is Matt here?" They shook their heads. The reaction was much the same at the second dressing room.

Outside, they found Matt's equipment bag in the back of the Jeep.

Keely interviewed the members of Matt's team and then the opposition. No one had seen him arrive. No one had seen him leave.

Lane found himself standing outside the front doors staring at the Jeep where it was parked under a street lamp.

A uniformed officer parked his car behind the Jeep.

What am I going to say to Arthur?

The officer got out of the cruiser and tied yellow tape around the light pole, then tied the tape to the mirror of the cruiser. He moved to the left. In another minute, the Jeep was bordered by a triangle of tape.

I saw Zander's body in that hole.

The officer looked at Lane and nodded as if to say, *We're with you on this one.*

I saw what happened to Lionel Birch.

Keely walked up and said, "We've talked to all of the players and the guy who works the rink."

Lane closed his eyes. When he opened them, he asked, "Are your mother, father, brother and Dylan okay?"

Keely nodded. "All okay."

Lane looked east toward the traffic whispering down the hill and into the river valley. Beyond that, a vehicle accelerated. The silver sedan growled up the incline.

He waited. The noise of the accelerating vehicle faded.

Keely asked, "You okay?"

A quartet of cars slipped down the hill. He heard them push through the air. *You're dropping into the valley. Into Moreau's territory.* For an instant, the darkness folded over him. He found it difficult to breathe. He saw another body. A pair of cowboy boots. A tattoo on an arm. Lane closed his eyes and breathed.

Keely said, "My dad was happy to hear from me."

"Good."

"The message is clear," Keely said.

"Which message is that?"

"Moreau's message. We're supposed to back off because we're getting too close. Pike got killed and it spooked Moreau. That's the message he sent us." Keely looked in the direction of the traffic. "What are you looking at?"

Lane shrugged. "Nothing."

"What will you do to Moreau?" Keely asked.

"First we get Matt and Jessica back, then..." Lane started and then found he could not complete the sentence.

"What's the next step?"

"I need to get some money out of the bank." Lane walked to the car.

Keely followed. "What's the money for?"

Lane got into the car and waited.

Keely got in behind the wheel.

"I need to buy some phones." Lane put on his seat belt.

"What's the plan?"

"Communications that can't be traced." Lane's phone rang. He plucked it from his pocket.

"Uncle Lane?" Christine asked.

"Yes." *There's terror in her voice.*

Keely accelerated and headed toward the city centre.

"What's wrong?" Christine asked.

"Tell me what happened." Lane watched the speedometer as Keely accelerated to one hundred.

"Somebody phoned Uncle Arthur."

Keely passed a truck pulling two trailers. The roar of the diesel engine momentarily filled the inside of the Chev.

"Well?" Lane asked.

Christine's words came out in a rush. "He said, 'Tell your boyfriend to back off.' What's it mean? We tried to phone Matt, but he's not answering."

Lane looked at his watch. "I'll be home in less than an hour. Are Dan and Arthur there with you at home?"

"Yes! And Roz too."

"Stay at home. Lock the doors. I'm on the way," Lane pressed end, dialed a number and put the phone back to his ear. "McTavish?"

"That's correct."

Lane recognized the deep baritone. "Lane here. I need a patrol car at my home. Officers you can trust."

"Right away, Detective Lane. What's happened?" McTavish asked.

"Someone's abducted my nephew." Lane pressed end.

After a brief stop at a bank machine, Lane returned with a wad of cash. He stuffed the bills into his jacket pocket. When he got into the car he said, "Take me home."

"How are you keeping so cool?"

"I'm not."

Keely frowned. "You could have fooled me."

"I have to focus on the moment and getting them both back. If I think about anything else . . ." Lane looked out the window. "Just get me home."

Keely looked ahead as the light turned. "We need to talk with Saadiq."

"Who?" Lane asked.

"Shit! Saadiq, my brother. Do you need a driver or a

partner?" Keely closed her mouth before she could say more.

"What are you talking about?"

"Are you going to let me in on your plans?"

Lane took a breath as rage threatened to engulf him. *Think!*

"Saadiq can help with the phones, and we can trust him. My brother has some friends."

"Some friends?" *We can't let too many people in on this.*

"Yes, people he trusts. People who know about Moreau and want to see him fall."

"Explain."

"People like Moreau think they're entitled because they're born here. Moreau and his crowd don't much like first- and second-generation Canadians like me." Keely eased the car into the left lane and accelerated. "Some of us have a pretty good idea about what Moreau is up to because lots of immigrants clean his restaurants and empty his garbage. A few of us even do some of his dirtier work."

"Saadiq's friends work for Moreau?" Lane asked.

"One of them has a cleaning contract for one of Moreau's restaurants."

Lane looked at her. He tried to smile. "Can I be your partner?"

"After I drive you home, I'll set up a meeting with Saadiq and his friends."

"After that we have another man to meet."

Fifteen minutes later, they walked into the front door of Lane's home. Arthur met them at the front door. He was a wet towel wrapped around Lane.

Christine stared at them from the couch where she sat next to a wide-eyed Daniel.

Roz stood on her back legs and rested her paws on Lane's thigh. She whimpered. He reached down and rubbed her behind the ears. Roz turned her head and licked the back of his hand. Her wagging tail twisted her off balance and she dropped back onto all fours.

"Where would they take Matt?" Arthur asked.

Keely answered. "That's what we need to find out."

Christine leaned forward to put her head in her hands. "They took Jessica too?"

"Looks like it," Keely said.

Daniel put his hand on Christine's back and rubbed between her shoulder blades.

"Harper wants you to get packed so we can get you somewhere safe," Lane said.

Arthur stepped back from Lane. Christine lifted her head.

Arthur said, "I think we'll stay here. We might as well be cooped up at home rather than someplace else. Besides, if we're here, we can help you get them back."

×

Mary sat in one of the women's shelter's second-hand rocking chairs and looked down at a sleeping Joshua. She gently combed her fingers through his thickening hair. It seemed to get longer every day. He took a deep breath. She stood, walked over to the crib, set him down and covered him with his blanket, one of the things she'd remembered to bring with them.

She looked around the room at the desk with initials carved into it, the dresser with decals on it and the single bed pushed up against the wall. Mary listened. A baby cried somewhere down the hall. A toilet flushed. She looked out the window and down to the street. Cars were parked on either side of the pavement. Mature trees touched branches over the middle of the road. The streetlight cast a soft glow over the shelter's empty sidewalk and private front yard.

So easy to escape, she thought. *All I had to do was ask the woman driving the bus how to get to the women's shelter and here we are.* She sat on the bed and watched Joshua breathe.

I need a plan, a way to get him out of this mess. Then she thought about Russell. *I hope he's okay.* The woman who had admitted Mary and Joshua to the shelter had taken one look at her swollen nose and said, "I don't want you to contact anyone. It's safer for you and your son. And it's safer for the other women in the shelter."

×

"Saadiq's business is all the way out here?" Lane asked as they travelled south along Deerfoot Trail.

"Yes, he's waiting for us. It's after closing." Keely eased off the freeway and headed east. She turned down a street where small industries and businesses had their parking lots out front.

After two kilometres, she turned north into a cul-de-sac and parked out front of Saliba's Deli.

They got out of the Chev and stepped inside the deli. "Saady?" Keely called.

Saadiq pushed through the swinging door behind the glass display of meats on one side, desserts in the middle and fresh veggies on the other side. He looked Lane in the eye. "So, I finally get to sit down with Detective Lane." Saadiq came around the counter, hugged his sister and offered his hand to Lane. Keely's brother had black hair, a thick five o'clock shadow, a straight nose and a smile that invited friendly conversation.

Keely pulled away from her brother. "We need some help."

"So you told me on the phone." Saadiq walked to the door, locked it and turned off the OPEN sign. He turned to Lane. "Kevin Moreau took your nephew and your friend's daughter."

You're putting Matt and Jessica's lives in his hands. Lane looked at Keely as he said, "That's correct."

"You need secure communications?" Saadiq studied Lane.

"That's right." Lane sat down at a nearby table.

Saadiq pulled a phone out of his shirt pocket, dialed and then put it on speaker and set it on the table in front of Lane.

"Hey, Ben, I need the best secure phone you've got." Saadiq lifted his chin at Lane. "How many do you need?"

Lane looked at Keely.

"How many? Be on the safe side." Saadiq sat down and leaned closer to the phone. "We'll be just a moment, Ben."

"Ten," Lane said and looked at Keely.

She raised her eyebrows.

"Make it twenty."

"How soon?" Ben asked.

"Right now if you can."

"Give me thirty minutes." Ben hung up and Saadiq stuffed the phone in his shirt pocket.

"Who's Ben?" Lane asked.

"A friend." Saadiq down across from Lane and asked, "You want a cup of coffee? We've got a few minutes."

Keely sat down with them. "Coffee would be nice."

Saadiq went in the back and called, "How about something to eat?"

Keely raised her eyebrows and looked at Lane. "That would be nice, too."

"The usual?" Saadiq asked.

"Sure." Keely looked out the window.

"I know why I've never really sat down with your brother."

"He went one way and I went another." Keely shrugged. "He's my family."

"What's he into?" Lane asked.

"Nothing anymore. We told him to stop. He stopped. He just kept his old friends who still dabble in this and that." Keely watched her brother through the display glass. "Some of his friends have connections with people who do odd jobs for Moreau. But they're friends of Saadiq's first."

"Lucky for Matt and Jessica."

"Very." Keely smiled and nodded.

The door to the kitchen swung open and Saadiq appeared. "Coffee's brewing. Give it five minutes." He put two falafels on the table, one in front of his sister and the other in front of Lane.

"How much do you know about Moreau's operation?" Lane asked.

Saadiq sat down. "A few bits and pieces."

"Give us what you have, Saady. Maybe some of your pieces will fit together with ours." Keely took a bite of her falafel. She closed her eyes. "Man, you still make the best in the city."

"Much of Moreau's operation involves relatives and one or two close friends. He usually uses aunts, uncles and cousins to deliver and pick up for him." Saadiq looked past Lane as if checking for traffic.

"From where?" Lane lifted his falafel. He inhaled the distinctive aromas of cabbage, tomatoes, sesame seeds, pickled beets, garlic, chickpeas and sweet red peppers.

"West coast. Some farms north of here. A few acreages to the south. Grow-ops in towns and cities." Saadiq watched a vehicle drive past. "Let's go in the back. Anybody driving up this road can see us if we sit out here." He led the way into the back where a small table was tucked among the stoves, stainless steel counters and walk-in fridge and freezer.

Lane smelled coffee brewing.

"You know that Moreau thinks he has power over you as long as your nephew and the child are alive?" Saadiq asked.

Lane chewed and covered his mouth. "Yes, and we need to move quickly. Moreau's a killer. Lately he's been pretty busy at it."

"And he has been killing for years. A very charming killer. Have you ever met him?" Saadiq asked.

"Yes, and so has Keely." Lane swallowed. *I'm starved and this is delicious.*

Saadiq turned to Keely. "Where?"

"When I worked undercover at the restaurant, and again the other day at a house he's building," Keely said.

"Stay away from him. He'll smile in your face, then stab you in the heart." Saadiq made a stabbing motion for effect.

"Or shoot you between the eyes," Keely said. "He used to have this expression when people asked him how he was doing. He'd say, 'Just chillin', not killin'.' Everybody else thought he was joking. I was never sure."

"He probably meant it both ways," Lane said.

"Hey! I forgot. I got some information from Hussein. He sells cars at a dealership in the northwest," Saadiq said.

Keely laughed. "Now he sells cars. You've got to be kidding!"

Saadiq ignored her laughter. "He told me that every two years some of Moreau's relatives come in and buy new pickup trucks from him. They pay cash. Their used trucks have major kilometres on them. When he comments on it, they always tell him their trucks get lots of highway travel."

"Proof of Moreau's delivery system?" Lane asked.

"Exactly. All you have to do is follow the trucks," Saadiq said.

"I'm surprised the Hells Angels haven't tried to move in on the operation." Keely used a napkin to wipe her mouth. "That really hit the spot, Saady."

Saadiq nodded thoughtfully. "The bikers and Moreau have a deal. They don't interfere with each other's operations so that everybody makes money. You know Moreau, he can sweet-talk anybody. Apparently some of the guys he went to school with became Angels. Even they don't want to mess with him as long as he maintains the status quo."

Ben walked into the back room fifteen minutes later. His brown hair was cut short. He filled up the doorway with his wide shoulders and thick biceps. He wore a yellow T-shirt and green shorts. He looked at Saadiq. "How's it goin', man?"

"Hey, Ben," Keely said.

"Hey, Keely. Where do you want me to put these?" Ben held up a plastic bag.

"Right here, man." Saadiq held out his hand.

Ben handed him the bag and Keely brought another chair over. "This is Lane."

"Good to meet you." Ben shook Lane's hand and sat down.

"Want something to eat?" Saadiq asked.

"You kidding? I love your falafels," Ben said.

Within a few minutes, Ben was eating and Saadiq was pouring more coffee.

"How much do we owe you, man?" Saadiq put the coffee pot on the hot plate.

Lane reached into his pocket, pulled out the wad of cash and set it on the table in front of Ben.

Ben put down the falafel, wiped his hands with a paper napkin, counted out what he was owed and handed the rest back.

Lane took the cash, picked out a hundred-dollar bill, handed it back to Ben and then asked, "How do the phones work?"

"Let the poor guy eat," Keely protested.

"It's easy." Ben smiled, stuffed the cash in the pocket of his shorts, chewed and talked.

Another person walked into the room.

Lane recognized Dylan's angular face and blond hair.

Saadiq looked at his sister. "I told him there was trouble. He's here to help."

Keely stood up and hugged Dylan.

Lane, Saadiq and Ben moved to the front of the deli when Keely began to cry.

Saadiq turned off the lights. In the glow of the streetlight coming through the window he looked at Lane, raised his chin and asked, "How come you're different?"

"I'm not sure what you mean," Lane said.

"My sister says you've treated her with respect." Saadiq glanced at Ben, who was taking Lane's measure. "You come in here and you're respectful. Lots of people like you want people like me and Ben cleaning tables and serving coffee."

"What exactly are you trying to say?" Lane asked.

"People like Ben, me and Keely. Immigrants and children of immigrants. Lots of Canadians don't want to allow people like me to join the club. That's why Kev Moreau is successful, you know. He shares some of what he takes with the people in town who are supposed to know their place even when he's using them. That, and he makes sure they're scared shitless of him. I'd just like to know what makes you different?"

"I'd like to know that, too," Ben said.

Lane looked at their faces and saw nothing but honest interest. He shrugged. "I guess I've never understood that kind of thinking. I know what it's like not to fit in. It's made me look at most things in a slightly different way. That, and my grandfather used to tell me stories about the people who helped him out along the way."

Saadiq said, "You look after my sister."

"I think Keely wants to look after herself," Lane replied.

Saadiq smiled. "We all need a little help from time to time."

Ben nodded and lifted the bag of phones to emphasize Saadiq's point. "They all have more minutes than you'll probably need. All have call display. If you think someone's listening in, throw that one away and use another one. I can program first names into them if you like."

Saadiq asked, "What exactly did you do to them?"

Ben shook his head. "I tweaked them a bit. You don't need to know any more. They're untraceable. Just do me a favour and return the ones you don't use. I keep a stash for emergencies."

×

Matt opened his eyes and looked at the ceiling. Light filled the room from a window above his head.

His right hand was asleep. Matt lifted his head and saw that his wrist was tied with blue nylon webbing — just like his feet.

He tasted burnt plastic. He swallowed. He closed his eyes.

"I'm gonna be sick," he said. His stomach heaved. "I'm gonna puke!"

The door opened. A man filled the doorway. He wore a red shirt, black jeans and a red devil mask. A muffin top hung over his belt. There was a black leather holster and the black grip of a pistol on his hip. The devil asked, "What's the matter?"

"I'm going to throw up." Matt noted two extra clips of ammunition in pouches attached to the devil's belt.

"Take a few deep breaths," the devil said.

"I tried that." Matt swallowed hard.

The devil pulled out a knife, flicked it open, leaned over Matt, released one hand and then the other.

Matt sat up. His hands began to tingle as the feeling returned. The tingling turned to pain.

The devil stepped back, drew his pistol and said, "Undo your feet."

Matt undid the knot. His fingertips clawed dumbly at the webbing at first, then succeeded in loosening the nylon.

When Matt finished, the devil said, "It's on your right. Leave the door open."

Matt tried to walk but stumbled into the wall.

The devil waited.

Matt leaned against the wall with his right shoulder to support him as he shuffled down the hall.

He turned on the light in the bathroom and knelt on the floor. He lifted the lid.

He heard a child's voice. "Matt?"

Jessica! His stomach heaved and he vomited.

chapter 11

Matt woke to a child crying in the adjacent bedroom. He opened his eyes and studied the room he was in. The walls and ceiling were beige. There was a closet with no doors. The window faced north, and reflected sunlight illuminated the floral curtains. He slept on a single mattress set atop a light-brown nylon carpet.

He turned to study the door. The hinges were on the outside. There was a deadbolt lock above the doorknob. He licked his lips. *God, I need to pee.*

He looked at the contusions on his wrists and wondered where the nylon webbing had gone.

The child's crying was a constant wailing, a wounded sound.

He sat up with his back against the wall. He used his elbows to pound against the drywall.

The crying went on uninterrupted.

The deadbolt lock slid open.

Matt turned to face the door.

The doorknob turned, and the devil's head looked down on him. "Need to take a leak?"

"Yes." Matt stood and then leaned against the wall when whirlpools of nausea made his head spin. After a moment, it cleared and he walked out of the bedroom.

The sound of crying was magnified as he walked by the doorway on his right.

The devil followed Matt, pounded on the door as he passed and yelled, "Shut up!"

The crying slowed. A child's voice said, "I want my daddy!"

It is Jessica, Matt thought. He looked down the hall at the TV. A baseball player stood up to the plate. A pair of wireless headphones sat on a coffee table.

"Come on. Leave the bathroom door open," the devil said.

Matt thought, *Sit down and think!* Jessica began to cry again.

The devil leaned his back against the wall. "That fuckin' kid!"

Matt dropped his pants, sat down and thought. *If Jessica's crying is driving this guy crazy, then use it.*

"Hurry up!" The devil looked down the hall at the TV and the headphones.

Take your time and see what happens.

The devil turned to Matt. "You said you needed to take a fuckin' leak!"

Matt dropped his head and looked at the beige linoleum. *On the way back to your room, make your move.*

"Hurry up, goddammit!" the devil said.

Matt reached for the handle on the toilet tank and flushed. He pulled up his pants and washed his face and hands. *Take your time! He'll get edgier.*

"Come on!" The devil put his hand on the grip of his pistol.

Matt stepped through the doorway.

The devil looked at Jessica's door.

Matt said, "I could keep her quiet for you."

"What?" the devil asked.

"Put her in the same room as me, and I'll keep her quiet."

The devil kept his hand on the butt of his gun. He took a moment to consider. "No funny stuff?"

Matt shook his head and looked at the floor. "No."

The devil stepped back so that Matt could enter his room. Matt stepped inside.

The devil's hand shoved Matt between the shoulder blades.

The door locked behind Matt. The crying intensified, then stopped. A minute later, Matt heard the sound of a key in the lock again. He stood up.

The door opened and Jessica was pushed inside.

"No funny stuff!" the devil warned.

"Matt?" Jessica grabbed Matt around the thighs and hugged him.

"I said none of that!" The devil bolted the door.

Five minutes later, Jessica was asleep in Matt's arms. She slept with her right hand in his. He used his sleeve to wipe the tears and snot from her face. Her hair was matted. She wore a denim jumper and a pink T-shirt with a princess holding a wand. Her shoes flashed pink when they touched any surface. Even in sleep she was never completely still.

Matt closed his eyes. A train rattled along the river valley. *It must be around seven in the morning. Remember, at home the train horn sounds around seven.* He leaned his head back and closed his eyes.

"Matt?" Jessica asked and squeezed his hand.

Matt opened his eyes and looked at her. "It's okay, Jessica. Go back to sleep." *How does she sense when I close my eyes?*

Jessica's hand relaxed in his.

He looked at her silver ear stud. *She nagged her mom for six months before Erinn finally gave in and got Jessica's ears pierced.*

He licked his lips. *Whatever they gave me made my mouth so dry.* He looked up at the deadbolt lock. *Be patient. Just be ready when the chance comes.*

×

"We've been given paid leave. The chief says we're too close to this." Harper wore a black running suit and shoes. He sat across from Lane and next to Keely in Central Blends, just on the edge of downtown. The coffee shop had expanded into what used to be an adjacent ice cream parlour.

"All three of us?" Keely wore her working clothes: a dark suit jacket and slacks.

"Lane and me." Harper pointed at his chest.

"So, what are you going to do next?" Keely asked.

"Find Jessica and Matt." Harper gave her an enigmatic glance that made Keely uncomfortable.

"What else would we do?" Lane wore his charcoal jacket, a red tie and grey slacks.

"First thing we're going to do is move to the other side of the coffee shop." Keely nodded at Elaine, the red-haired barista behind the counter.

"It's all yours," Elaine said.

"What are you up to?" Lane got up with his coffee in one hand and a canvas bag in the other.

"Lori and I will be your department connection. That is assuming, of course, that you two want to be involved in the operation?" Keely picked up her cup, stood and walked through the doorway leading to the other side of the coffee shop.

Lane followed. "What operation?"

Keely sat on a bench where five tables ran along the south wall beneath black-and-white photographs taken in Nepal.

Lane sat down across from her. Harper sat next to him.

"How many phones do you have?" Keely asked.

"You know how many phones I have," Lane said.

"Set them on the table, please." Keely opened her purse.

Lane reached down for the canvas bag. He felt Harper's hand on his arm.

"What's the plan, Saliba?" Harper asked.

"You need manpower. We've got a number of cases to solve: the murders of Zander Rowe, Lionel Birch, Roberta King and Stan Pike. It's likely that if we solve one, we'll solve all of them. Right now, though, the priority for you two is finding Matt and Jessica. With the complexities involved, we need more people. Saadiq is only one man. He has lots of connections, but he's not enough."

Lane turned at the sound of a voice from the other room.

"Do you have soy milk for that?" Christine asked.

Lane took in all that he saw and shook his head. "No. Not them."

Harper agreed. "No way."

"Listen to what they have to say and then decide," Keely said.

Harper stood up. "It's too dangerous."

Keely grabbed him by the wrist. "Listen to what they have to say."

Harper winced, and she released her grip. He sat back down, shaking his wrist.

It took ten minutes for all of the tea, coffee and muffins to arrive. By that time, ten bodies were gathered around three tables shoved together to form a wobbly square.

"How did you get here?" Harper asked his wife Erinn, who sat next to him.

She rubbed her extended belly. "I parked at one end of the shopping mall up on the hill. Then I caught a taxi here."

"You?" Lane asked Christine and Daniel.

Daniel said, "We rode the LRT. No one got off at the stop except the two of us. So we just walked down the hill."

Arthur said, "I drove downtown, parked at City Hall and got a ride here with Lori."

"We were careful, but not as cautious as he was." Lori nodded at Glenn, nephew of Harper and Erinn.

Glenn's usually carefully gelled hair was stuck to his scalp. "I rode my bike."

"There's no way this can work. It's too dangerous," Harper said.

Lane nodded. "I don't like it."

"I don't like it either. Someone thinks he can take Matt

and Jessica and get away with it? No way," Christine said. She had a tiny white moustache from the soymilk foam on top of her latte.

Erinn put her coffee down. She took a breath but her voice still shook. "Quite frankly —" she pointed at Harper and Lane "— this isn't your call. Uniformed officers are watching both of our houses. They're gonna be pissed at me because I ditched them. So what? They'll get over it. I want my daughter back." She pointed at Lane and Arthur. "You want Matt back. Jessica will be scared. I want her back sooner rather than later. Stop the bullshit and give me a job to do."

"What's my job gonna be? I want my brother back," Christine said.

Lane opened his mouth to answer and closed it when he realized that she'd called Matt her brother. *That's a first.*

"I'll coordinate with Lori," Arthur said.

"How will we communicate?" Glenn asked.

This time Arthur reached for the phones. "Each one has its number taped on the back. Under that are the names and numbers assigned to each of the other phones." He picked one out and read the label. "This one's yours, Erinn." He handed it to her. "Keep your phones with you at all times. And make sure they're always charged."

"When did you do this?" Lane asked.

"While you slept last night." Arthur handed a phone to Harper. "All of our numbers are on speed dial on each phone. Still, I suggest we memorize all ten numbers as soon as possible. And if you think your phone has been compromised, let someone know. We've got more."

"You've got it all planned out already?" Harper asked.

Keely said, "Not all of it. We need you two to work out our first move. Arthur is running the command centre out of his house."

×

There was a tapping on Mary's door. She checked on Joshua, who had just fallen asleep again after a restless night. Then she got to her feet and opened the door.

A black-haired woman stood there. She wore a pair of blue working gloves, a sky-blue cotton sweatsuit, rubber boots and a tight perm. She asked, "You the girl who's running from Kev Moreau?"

Mary looked down at her own borrowed T-shirt, grey flannel pajama bottoms and red toenails.

"I'm Rita, and I wanna keep an eye on you if that's okay." She backed up a step as if sensing Mary needed some space and time to think.

"How do you know about me?" Mary put her hands on her hips.

"I volunteer as a gardener. Sometimes people who work here talk and forget their windows are open." Rita cocked her head to the left.

"Why do you care?" Mary asked.

"Moreau hurt my niece real bad when she was in high school. She left school, left the country and ended up working for MSF. I haven't seen her in more than ten years. He did something to her. Something she doesn't talk about. Something she's spent the last few years trying to make up for. She was my favourite, you see. Now she has a son of her own. A little boy she adopted the day he was born. Someday I hope to meet him. Maybe they'll come home for a visit or maybe I'll go and see them. Anyway, I just wanted you to know I'll be looking out for you and your little boy. If you feel like going outside, the backyard is real private. I won't bother you again unless you decide you wanna talk. The next move's up to you." Rita turned and walked down the hall and down the stairs.

Mary closed the door then checked to see whether Joshua was still asleep. *What's MSF? If this woman knows I'm here, who else knows?*

"It's not a problem, trust me." Kev Moreau sat behind the five-centimetre-thick glass table he'd bought for photo opportunities. It was meant symbolize the new transparency he wished to portray to the city's more patrician citizens. He wore a black suit, white shirt and blue tie. "I know you had nothing to do with what happened to Stan." He indicated with an open hand that Russell should sit down. The cuff of Kev's shirt displayed his embroidered initials.

Russell did as he was instructed. "I don't know where they went. I've been calling her family, everyone we know. They've disappeared." He looked at his hands as if they could offer him some answers.

"They'll turn up." Kev appeared to be looking at the ceiling.

Russell felt compelled to break the silence. "What was Stan doing at my house, anyway?"

Kev dropped his chin and his eyes. "Don't know. Stan was kind of a loose cannon."

Stan Pike did only what you told him to do, Russell thought.

"We just need to keep our cool and keep our mouths shut. You can do that, can't you?" Moreau's words carried an undertone of threat.

Russell nodded automatically. *That's what I've done for the last ten years. What have you done with Joshua and Mary?* "Don't worry about me, Kev. I know how to keep a secret."

✕

Former Gang Member Turns to Philanthropy

Self-confessed former gang member and long-time city resident Kevin Moreau revealed plans to sign over the title of a west-side apartment building. Residents are asking why.

"People in this community supported me when I was growing up. It's time for me to give back," Moreau announced at a news conference at his flagship restaurant, Kev's. Moreau plans to offer ownership opportunities to the residents of his fourteen-storey apartment building. Individual units will be signed over to long-time tenants provided they have been residents in good standing.

"I'm rewarding long-time tenants because they are the kind of people who work hard but will never be able to afford a place of their own," Moreau explained. "I've done well by this community and it's time to share my good fortune."

The apartment building overlooks the river and a city park.

The mayor welcomed the news, saying, "The city is behind Mr. Moreau's plan. Affordable housing is an issue in this city, and Mr. Moreau is offering a workable solution."

Moreau plans to hand over ownership of the apartments to residents at a New Year's Eve ceremony.

"Where do we start?" Keely drove west along the river valley. On the sidewalk to the left, a woman in a skin-tight, multi-coloured synthetic outfit jogged behind a stroller. It was a metre-wide, chrome-plated affair. She forced cyclists, walkers and joggers off the pavement while listening to music only she could hear.

"How many cases do we have to solve?" Lane sat in the back seat.

"Explain?" Harper sat next to him.

"Zander Rowe, Lionel Birch, Roberta King, Stan Pike and the kidnapping of Jessica and Matt," Lane said.

"I think we're working on one. We solve Zander's case, and we'll know what happened in each of the other cases." Keely changed lanes and turned right to head north toward the hospital.

"What about Mary Lowell and the baby? What's its name?" Harper asked.

"Joshua."

"That's right. Baby Joshua may have been Moreau's third bit of insurance, after Jessica and Matt. If we're being told to back off or Matt and Jessica will be hurt, then who is being warned by having Joshua taken away?" Lane asked.

"Do you think Mary's husband Russell knows something?" Harper asked.

"So, we're working on the assumption that Matt and Jessica are all right?" Keely asked.

"I'm working on that assumption." Lane looked at Harper.

Harper looked out the window. "You think Fibre will help us?"

Lane's phone rang. He pulled the burner phone out of his pocket. "Hello."

Harper watched Lane.

Keely stopped at a red light. She too was watching Lane in the rear-view mirror.

Lane nodded and ended the call. "Arthur got another message on our home phone. The caller said, 'Back off the Rowe case, and the boy and the girl will be released in a week. Otherwise, the devil takes his mask off.' Word for word."

Harper nodded and continued to look out of the window.

"What do we do?" Keely asked.

"Find Matt and Jessica and solve the murders," Lane said.

"Aren't you guys worried about your jobs if you don't stay out of this?" Keely asked.

Lane and Harper looked at each other. Both said, "No."

Harper said, "The last thing the chief said to me before I left his office was, 'Wear your vest and tell the other two to do the same.' So — if I read between the lines — he can tell everyone else we're on leave, but he knows we'll be working to solve this one. He can't tell us to keep working on the case, but he's given us the time to concentrate on it."

"Okay, then. Where do we meet Fibre?" Keely asked.

Ten minutes later, Fibre walked up the slope of the car park on the north side of the Foothills Medical Centre. He held a paper bag in his hand.

Lane pointed at the passenger side of the front seat.

Fibre got in. "This is unusual. Why are you meeting me here, and why is Deputy Chief Harper here?"

"We're supposed to ask the questions." Lane tried to smile.

Fibre opened his lunch bag, looked around him and closed the bag.

You've taken Fibre out of his comfort zone. Go easy. Lane said, "We were hoping you could give us a forensic update on Stan Pike."

Fibre nodded. "My lawyer said you gave me good advice. He said that you were right. Gaia's lawyer already sent the medical report. She is pregnant with triplets. We're in the process of confirming paternity, and I've chosen a realtor."

"What did she say about the house?" Lane asked.

"Actually, I proposed a duplex." Fibre turned in his seat so that his back was to the door.

Keely looked at Fibre like he'd just landed on the planet. Lane heard Harper inhale impatiently.

"So you can live in one side and she in the other?" Lane thought, *Let him tell his story first. He's obviously got to let this out before he can talk about the rest.*

Fibre nodded.

"Very clever. That way you can see the kids and live close to them at the same time." Lane smiled at the doctor.

Fibre nodded, smiled, looked at his lunch, appeared to remember why he was in the car and began to talk evidence. "The petroleum signature on Pike's effects was a match to a sample of accelerant found at the King residence. Mr. Pike's femoral artery was severed at an angle and exsanguination was the result. The fingerprints on the knife that killed Pike belong to a Mary Lowell. She was caught shoplifting a few years ago and processed."

"Anything else you can tell us?" Lane asked.

"No matches were found to the hair and fibre samples found at the Lionel Birch crime scene." Fibre opened his door. "But he was shot twice: once in the head and once in the heart. The same way Zander Rowe was killed."

"Will you call Detective Saliba with any other evidence?" Lane asked.

"Yes." Fibre climbed out of the car. He closed the door and walked down the ramp and out of the parkade.

"Where do you want to be dropped off? 'Cause where I'm going you can't go," Keely said.

"What does that mean?" Harper asked.

"It means," Lane said, "she's going to look for the missing Mary and her son. Keely thinks maybe Mary and the boy ended up hiding in a women's shelter. Keely figures two men tagging along will be a handicap. So you and I will track from another angle."

"Didn't know I was that transparent," Keely said.

"Can you drop us off near the Children's Hospital?" Harper asked.

Keely followed Harper's directions. She stopped in a graveled back alley behind the double garage of a sprawling bungalow. It sat on a lot big enough for two houses.

Lane and Harper got out and watched Keely drive out of the alley.

The dust of her departure hung in the air while Harper pulled a set of keys out of his pocket and walked alongside the grey-stuccoed garage. "Give me a second to open the door."

"Whose place is this?" Lane asked.

"My folks'. They're on holidays." Harper stopped at the side of the garage, stuck a key in the door lock and wiggled it up and down.

Lane waited in the alley and a minute later Harper opened the metal garage door. Light poured in. The smell of dust, oil and wood seeped out. A twenty-year-old pickup truck sat with its grill pointed toward Lane. "Does it run?"

Harper smiled. "Of course. And it should fit right in where we'll be going."

Harper climbed inside the cab. He fumbled with the keys.

Lane looked down one end of the alley and up the other.

The starter whined. Lane thought, *Just stay focused. Forget the what-ifs. Find Matt and Jessica and bring them home.*

The engine caught. Harper eased the truck out of the garage.

Lane saw a half moon of rust eating its way over the rear wheel well. He closed the garage door and climbed in the passenger side.

"How are you staying so cool?" Harper asked.

Lane fumbled between the cushions for the seat belt. "You should know me better than that."

"You're on the hunt, then?" Harper aimed the truck down the alley.

Lane nodded and finished putting on his seat belt.

"We need to agree on one thing."

"We're going to get Matt and Jessica home safe."

"Not just that." Harper stopped at the end of the alley.

"You mean about Moreau?" Lane asked.

"That's right," Harper said while he put the left signal light on. "We agree that Moreau will not walk away from this one. If we have to take care of him, then we do it."

"Understood." *It's so easy to go over to the other side — the dark side.*

"He won't come after our kids again," Harper said.

"No."

"Where do we start?" Harper asked.

"Lori and Arthur are working on a list of Moreau's properties. When we have that, we narrow the list down. Then we watch for pizza deliveries," Lane said.

"Pizza?"

"Matt loves pizza and so does Jessica. It'll be a signal," Lane said.

Harper stopped at a red light. "You're joking, right?"

"You remember a couple of weeks ago, we ordered pizza?" Lane asked.

"Of course. Jessica ate her weight in it." The engine began to run rough. Harper tapped his foot on the accelerator. The engine smoothed itself out.

"That was the special from Florence Pizza. It's the only one in town. In fact it's right in the middle of Kev's neighbourhood. I know the owner. He's a relative of Uncle Tran. We can trust him because of that. Once we have a list of Moreau's properties, we wait until a Florence Special pizza is ordered from one of Moreau's addresses." Lane looked ahead.

"So, we're gambling their lives on a pizza?" The engine died. Harper restarted the truck.

"Matt's smart and he loves pizza. He'll manage to send us that signal somehow. If not, we have a backup," Lane said.

"Well?"

"The kidnapper will need to have food delivered. It's a safe bet Moreau will use his relatives to do the deliveries. Saadiq is preparing a list of the vehicles owned by Moreau's delivery team. The only problem is we have to know which property to watch first." Lane looked out his window. Two kids were aiming water guns at one another. Both fired at the same time.

"So Saadiq's friend will tell us which vehicles to watch out for?"

"Exactly." Lane grabbed his phone and dialed.

×

"I'm hungry," Jessica said.

Matt got off the bed and knocked on the door. He waited.

Footsteps approached from the kitchen. The devil said, "Yep."

Matt thought, *Keep it short. Don't give him much.* "We're hungry."

"It's on the way," said the voice behind the devil mask.

He's got to sleep sometime. "Bathroom break."

"After you eat. You know the rules."

Matt looked at Jessica, who was sucking her thumb. He smiled at her. She waved at him without removing her thumb. He reached down and checked the sock on his right foot. *My phone is gone. Of course it's gone.* He caught a whiff of his armpit. *And I'm beginning to smell.*

Jessica took her thumb out of her mouth and said, "Stinky."

"How about a shower too?" Matt asked.

×

"Rita, what does MSF stand for?" Mary sat on the step overlooking the backyard of the women's shelter. Joshua squirmed on her knee.

Rita was on her hands and knees pulling a thistle out of a bed of blue flax. "It's the organization my niece works for." Rita grunted, the thistle's root let go and she fell backwards to sit on the grass. "*Médecins sans frontières*. It's a French name. It means 'doctors without borders.' They go around to places in the world where people need help. MSF stays out of the politics and sets up medical care."

"How come she left the city?" Mary set Joshua down on the grass. He looked at a dandelion and leaned over to pick it. "Do you spray the dandelions?"

Rita looked over her shoulder at the baby and smiled. "Nope. Thanks for the help there, Josh."

Joshua stuck the yellow flower in his mouth, then coughed, made a face and spat the yellow out.

Mary watched her son try a dandelion leaf. He chewed on one and picked another.

"It was that pervert Pike. He made a movie of my niece and Kev Moreau." Rita groaned as she got to her feet. She leaned on her shovel and looked at Mary.

Mary had heard the venom in Rita's voice. "A movie?"

"A porno. He made a movie of Candace and Kev having sex. Then he played it for some of his boys at her high school. She was devastated. You can imagine. Candy wouldn't go back to school. Some of the teachers got together and made it so she could graduate. Then my sister sent her away to university. Somehow, the school got her scholarships so she could afford an education. A teacher named King made it all happen. Candace hasn't been back to this city since."

"There's more, isn't there?" Mary asked.

Rita looked at Mary.

Mary picked Joshua up and pulled a leaf out of his mouth.

"Promised Candace I'd never talk about it."

A window slid open on the second floor.

Rita looked up and spotted one of the other women at the window. Rita put her head down and walked up to Mary. "Let me show you some flowers on this side of the house." She pretended to look up. "That's Dee Dee Tee. A regular around here. A regular pain in the ass who always ends up goin' back to the guy who beats her. She's always listenin' in for juicy bits of gossip. Don't trust her one bit."

Mary stood up and followed.

Between the fence and the building, flowering plants — including nasturtiums, blue flax and marigolds — grew tightly planted next to one another.

Rita turned to face the younger woman. "Just watch what you say. Moreau has offered an apartment for anyone who locates you. So you need to keep yourself under wraps. Don't tell anyone your name."

Mary hugged Joshua closer. "Pike tried to take my son."

Rita nodded. "Mr. Pike won't be doing that again. And he won't be makin' no more movies neither. I feel like I owe you one because of what Pike and Moreau did to my niece. You took care of Pike. He had it comin' and so does Moreau."

"What else did Moreau and Pike do?"

A woman with a sleeveless top and right arm in a sling appeared at the side of the house. She stared at Mary and Rita.

Rita waved at the woman and turned her back. "We'll have to talk about that later."

Arthur sat on the edge of the couch and looked at the posters he had arranged on the living room wall. Each poster listed a separate property or business owned by Kev Moreau. Next to those he had a list of the license plates, makes, models and colours of vehicles owned by Moreau's relatives. Another chart was blank and waiting for information that did not fit under the other headings.

He sat back and began flipping his thumb through a pad of sticky notes. He looked at the other packages of notes that came in a variety of colours. Roz sat beside him. She looked at the wall. Arthur looked at some of his notes on his right. Then he looked at the article in the paper. "How come ten percent of those apartments are unoccupied?"

Roz looked at him and tilted her head to the right.

"What did you say?" Christine stepped out of the kitchen with a glass of water. She sat next to Arthur and looked at the wall.

He pointed at the middle poster. "Ten percent of those apartments have been empty for the last three years."

"Are they all on one floor?"

"Good question. I'll find out." Arthur picked up his phone, dialed and asked, "Lori? Arthur here. Could you please use your contacts at City Hall and Enmax to find out if the power bills on one floor of Kev Moreau's apartment building are lower than the others?"

After he finished the call he turned to Christine. "It's fortunate that Moreau's building bills each resident for power. We're going for lunch."

"Where?" Christine asked.

"Chinatown. Uncle Tran's place. I need to talk with him." Arthur reached for his car keys.

"Daniel will drive us," Christine said.

"Daniel?" Arthur turned to look at her.

"He's using his parents' car. It's less conspicuous. We don't want the wrong people spotting us whenever we go somewhere." Christine walked over and stood at the top of the stairs leading to the family room. "We're ready, Dan!"

Daniel came up the stairs. "Where are we off to?"

✕

"Haven't seen Mary in five years," Lauren O'Connor said.

Keely looked down the hallway. O'Connor was a bleached-blonde anorexic wearing a grey housecoat. She floated in a cloud of mouthwash, chewing gum, peppermint and alcohol. "Does she stay in contact with you?" Keely asked.

The woman shook her head. "No."

How is it possible to slur the word 'no'? "So, you have no idea where I'll find her or her baby?" She resisted the impulse to take a step back for a breath of fresh air.

"Baby?" O'Connor asked.

"That's right."

"Bitch never told me I was a grandmother!"

"I just needed to confirm that Mary Lowell is your daughter." Keely took a step back. *If this was my mother, I'd keep my kid away from her too.*

"So she did marry that Russ Lowell. What an asshole! Always hanging around here, sniffing like a dog after a bitch in heat." Lauren leaned against the wall and looked at the floor. She gave the worn linoleum an accusatory glare.

"We're trying to find her and could use your help." Keely took out her card and set it on a ledge next to a plant with yellow, curled-up leaves.

Lauren laughed. The laugh turned into a cough. She lowered her head, put her hands on her knees, cleared her throat, and pulled a tissue from her sleeve. She spat into it, wrapped up the phlegm and tucked it into her pocket. "She doesn't come here, doesn't call. Too good for her poor mother."

"I don't blame her," Keely said.

"What did you say to me?"

Keely reached for her phone, dialed and spoke. "Arthur?" She turned her back on Lauren O'Connor and walked down the front steps.

"Who are you to judge me? What are you? You're just another fuckin' cop!"

Keely pulled her car keys from her pants pocket and walked down the front walk.

"Take your fuckin' card and shove it up your ass!"

"No sign of Mary or the baby at the mother's place." Keely shut the phone off and stuffed it in her jacket pocket as she approached the Chev.

Her phone rang as she settled behind the wheel. She checked the caller's ID and hesitated. "Dylan?"

"What can I do next to help?" Dylan asked.

Keely put her head in her left hand. "Arthur could use some help at his end. My RCMP supervisor is telling me that after this case I'm no longer on loan to the city police."

"Have you told Lane?" Dylan asked.

"No. Not yet. It's the wrong time."

"Can we get together later?"

Keely lifted her head and looked out the windshield. "Where?"

Uncle Tran's hair was entirely white. For a five-foot-tall man who weighed no more than one hundred twenty pounds, he managed to fill the room with his enormous presence. Tran smiled as Arthur followed Christine and Daniel into the Lucky Elephant Restaurant.

The smile disappeared.

Christine and Daniel allowed Arthur to pass them.

"There is a problem," Uncle Tran said.

Arthur nodded.

"Sit down. We will discuss this over lunch." Uncle Tran shook hands with Christine and Daniel. "Your family continues to grow." He smiled as he saw Daniel looking at Christine the way one lover looks at another.

Arthur sat down next to Tran. "In a way, that's why we're here."

"This Moreau is a cruel one." Tran poured tea for Arthur. "I've seen his kind before."

"My nephew, Matt is…" Arthur began but couldn't finish the sentence.

Tran held up his hand. "I know."

"How?" Christine asked.

Tran shrugged and poured her a cup. "People say things in restaurants thinking they will not be overheard."

"Do you know where he is?" Daniel asked.

"Not yet." Tran waved at one of the waiters. He said something in Vietnamese. The waiter moved to the door and locked it. He turned off the OPEN sign. Tran asked, "We will have a private conversation?"

"Thank you," Arthur said.

"Will you help us?" Christine asked.

"We are friends?" Tran asked.

Arthur smiled.

Christine said, "Yes, of course."

"Well, then how can I help? And after we discuss that, I will tell you what is already being done." Tran waved the waiter over. "First, we will have something to eat."

chapter 12

"You're not much good if you don't sleep." Harper sat in the driver's seat. They were parked a block away from Moreau's home. It was an all-brick, two-storey house backing onto the river. The wall around the property was nearly two metres high.

"Not all of us can fall asleep like you can." Lane sipped the coffee they'd picked up after a night of sitting in the truck. "How do you do it, anyway? You must have slept for four hours straight."

"I don't know. The more stressful it gets, the more I'm able to recharge. Anyway, Jessica is not at Moreau's place. No one has been in or out all night. And Arthur's got more promising leads."

"You sure?" Lane asked.

Harper nodded. "Yep." He reached for the key in the ignition. "We need another set of wheels. People around here will recognize this truck tomorrow." He started the engine.

×

Matt watched Jessica as she slept. She lay sprawled across the pillow, leaving a small corner for his head. From time to time during the night, she would kick him in the face. He took to sleeping with one arm tucked in front of his nose.

There was a knock on the apartment door. He heard footsteps and a wordless exchange. A minute later, there was the scent of fresh coffee. *Same routine as yesterday morning*, Matt thought. He could hear the rumble of the train heading west.

"Hey, kid."

"What?"

"Want a cup of coffee?" the devil asked.

"That would be nice." Matt watched the deadbolt slide back. The doorknob turned. The devil handed Matt a paper cup. The door closed. Matt sipped his coffee and waited. The deadbolt did not slide to anchor itself in the doorframe. Matt looked at Jessica and stared at the door. Then he looked at his cup and the cardboard heat sleeve. He looked at the wall. Reflected light was shining on the paint through a gap in the curtains. A rainbow the size of a business card had formed on the wall over Jessica's head. Her eyes opened. He took her hand and held it up to the wall. The rainbow was in the palm of Jessica's hand. She looked at her hand and smiled.

×

"Detective Saliba?"

Keely recognized the voice and felt tension run up her back. "Chief Simpson." She held the phone tightly, trying to interpret the formality in his voice. She gripped the steering wheel with her left hand and looked though the windshield. The Chev was parked with its front right tire nudged up against the curb. Four people stepped out of the coffee shop on Parkdale Boulevard. They sipped their cups and smiled.

"The body of a male in his late teens or early twenties was discovered this morning. The victim was dumped in a parking lot just below the Bearspaw Dam on the north side of the river. No ID on the body. I need you to attempt to identify the victim. This is top priority. Phone me back at this number."

Keely reached for the keys. *What's the quickest way there?*

"There's more," Simpson said.

"What now?"

"Robert Rowe is still at large and may be headed for Calgary."

You're telling me this why?

"It's a complication you need to be aware of. His description is being forwarded to you as we speak." Simpson hung up.

Ten minutes later, with lights flashing, Keely looked for the turnoff to the Trans-Canada Highway as she headed west toward the dam.

The Trans-Canada was a parking lot due to construction, so she turned down a residential street.

She approached a controlled intersection. The light was red. The vehicles in either lane parted to allow her through. She turned on the siren and nosed into the intersection.

A green import ran through the intersection. Keely jammed her foot on the brakes.

The other driver looked straight ahead. Keely caught a glimpse of a mother driving with a cell phone in one hand and the other raised off the wheel as an exclamation point. A child in a car seat stared open mouthed at the police car.

"Keep your eyes open." Keely checked to see that everyone else in the intersection had stopped. She followed the road to the right and headed for a second bridge over the Bow River.

×

"It's Arthur." He answered the phone while taking a fresh look at the charts on the wall.

"A young man's body has been found," the voice said.

Arthur heard electronic distortion in the man's voice.

"The face on the body has been badly damaged. It'll take time to identify him. Late teens. Black hair. Medium build. Sound familiar?" The voice hung up.

Arthur turned as the doorbell rang. He looked at the phone and then out the front-room window. Erinn held her hands protectively over her belly. He walked to the front door and opened it.

"You're pale. What's happened?" Erinn asked.

"Another warning."

A shiver went through her. "Jessica?"

"No," Arthur said. "It was about Matt."

Arthur looked past Erinn and saw Maria approaching the front door. She was wearing jeans, a white blouse and red oven mitts. She danced on the front step with a large pan. "It's hot. Can I put this in your kitchen?"

"Sure." Arthur stood to one side while Maria rushed past in an aromatic cloud of citric perfume, tomato sauce, Parmesan Romano cheese and garlic. He followed her into the kitchen.

Erinn ambled after them. "Is Matt okay?"

Maria set the dish on top of the stove. "You were so kind to help me out. I was making lasagna, so I made two batches." She turned to look at Erinn, who sat down carefully in a kitchen chair. "I'm Maria."

"Erinn." Her red hair was in need of a wash. There were dark half circles under her eyes.

Arthur stood next to the fridge. "Thank you for the food. It smells wonderful."

Christine pounded up the stairs. "Did they find Matt?" She landed on the kitchen floor, looked at Maria and stuck her hand over her mouth.

"I noticed the police officers patrolling the neighbourhood." Maria looked around the room at each of the three faces.

Daniel ran up the stairs to stand behind Christine. "Are they okay?" He saw Maria and blanched.

Maria looked at Arthur. "It seems that you and I are destined to meet at very awkward times."

Erinn wrapped her hands around her belly. "They took my daughter, Jessica. She's three. And they took Matt."

"Who are they?" Maria asked.

✕

Keely stopped as the gravel road opened up into a spacious lot lined with wooden telephone poles set on their sides to act as dividers.

A police cruiser and the Forensic Crime Scene Unit van were parked at the west end, closest to the dam. At the base of that solid wall of concrete, the water boiled deep, white and fast.

Next to the FCSU van, a body lay covered with a yellow tarp. Dr. Colin Weaver stood between Keely and the body. He was dressed in his white bunny suit. He held his hands at his sides as the detective got out of her car and approached the scene.

"I was hoping you could help us identify the body," Fibre said. "Actually, I was hoping you could tell me this isn't Detective Lane's nephew because he fits the description of Matthew Mereli: late teens, five foot ten, one hundred seventy pounds, black hair, brown eyes." Fibre hesitated, then added, "At least, I think his eyes are brown."

Keely felt drawn to the tarp. She wanted to be anywhere else but here, yet she felt she had to get closer to the body.

Fibre lifted a corner of the tarp. "The body was discovered by a couple out for a walk with their dog. There was no identification on the young man. And —" he pulled the tarp back fully "— he was shot at close range."

Keely crouched to get a closer look. Her knees cracked. She reached into her jacket pocket and brought out a pair of surgical gloves.

The victim had a third eye near the centre of his forehead, just above the eyebrows. Below the eyes, the face had been smashed. The teeth had obviously been knocked out. She lifted the tarp to see the hands. Each hand was a meaty stump relieved of fingers and thumbs.

Keely closed her eyes. *Think! Rely on your training. You know what to look for.* She lifted the tarp higher. Another bullet hole stained the victim's blue T-shirt. The hole was on the left side of the chest just over where the heart should lie. She stood and walked around the body. The sole of one black shoe was visible at the bottom edge of the yellow tarp.

"What do you see?" Fibre asked.

"One shoe." Keely lifted the tarp to inspect the feet. Both soles were so worn that the heels were free of tread.

"We may have to use DNA to identify him. That could take a week."

Keely studied the wear on the sole of the right shoe and then the left. "Matt has a mild form of cerebral palsy. These shoes look to be at least a couple of months old. The wear pattern is relatively even. Look at the heels."

Fibre came around to look over her shoulder. "Of course."

"Matt has a hitch to his walk. That means the wear pattern would be asymmetrical if this was him." Keely let the tarp drop.

"These wear patterns are symmetrical," Fibre said. She could hear the relief in his voice.

Fibre stepped back from the body. "If you don't think it's Matt, we will still have to check DNA and the victim's tattoo to find out who this is."

Keely looked at Fibre. "A tattoo?"

"Yes. On his back." Fibre stepped forward, lifted the tarp, rolled the body and lifted the blue T-shirt so that she could see the back of the victim's torso. A pair of monkeys eyed each other from opposite shoulder blades. In between them — next to the spine — was the tip of a bullet poking out of an opening in the skin.

Keely stepped back from the body.

Fibre gently rolled the body onto its back and re-covered it with the tarp. "Again, there are similarities to the Rowe and Birch killings. Both were shot once in the forehead and once in the heart."

Keely reached into her pocket for the phone.

"You will inform Detective Lane?"

Keely nodded. "Please do the ballistics match as quickly as possible. We need to know if the weapon and bullets are a match with any of the other victims."

Fibre nodded and waved his crew closer. "As soon as I get the body to the coroner and get back to the lab with the bullet."

×

Lane climbed out of the truck. He looked through the chain-link fence surrounding the city's impound lot.

Harper locked his door and pocketed the keys. "See anything you like?"

Lane nodded in the direction of a late-model Cadillac. There was a layer of black dust on the silver paint and windows, but what was under the grime looked intact.

Harper shook his head. "That one." He pointed at a green Jeep. "It'll go anywhere we need to go."

Lane's phone rang. He reached into his pocket grabbed the phone and put it to his ear. "Lane."

Harper mouthed, *Okay with you?*

Lane held his hand up. "That's right, he has cerebral palsy.... Yes, the soles of his shoes wear unevenly. We have to buy him new ones every three months or so.... No, no tattoos and certainly none depicting monkeys on his back." He nodded, closed the phone and looked at Harper. "The body isn't Matt. But it looks like Moreau sent us another message." He choked on the last word. He looked through the tears at Harper. *Not now*, Lane thought. *You can do this after Matt and Jessica are home and safe.* He took a long breath. "Okay, let's go with the Jeep."

×

Mary sat in the common room. Joshua slept in the crook of her arm with one hand on her breast. She looked at his angel face. Mary put her hand on his chest just to see whether he was still breathing. *You're perfect and you look so much like Russell. I hope he's okay,* she thought.

Mary heard a sound and looked up at a woman with long brown hair who was twice her age. She sported rainbow-bruised cheeks and a crooked nose that had met up with a fist on more than one occasion.

Mary nodded and thought, *She's wearing long sleeves today.*

"I'm Dee Dee," the woman said. Her tone of voice was overly sweet and there was something dark hiding behind her smile. She stepped closer and ran a fingernail down the baby's cheek.

Mary's protective instincts caused her to shiver. She stood. *Keep him away from Dee Dee!* "I'd better get him off to bed."

"Pretty baby." Dee Dee followed Mary. "I'm the resident social worker around here. Everybody talks to me. Shares their problems. You can talk to me any time you like. I'm even training to be a doula."

"What the hell is a doula?" Mary headed for the stairs.

"I'll work with mothers before and after they give birth."

Mary went upstairs, down the hall and opened the door to her room.

Dee Dee was a step behind. "We could talk right now. Maybe you need some postpartum support."

Mary turned and smiled. "He needs his sleep and so do I." She stepped inside her room, closed the door and locked it. She waited five minutes until she heard Dee Dee's retreating footsteps.

×

"I don't get it. You're all calm and cool. It's not like you to be this way," Christine complained.

Arthur looked at her, tried to speak but found that he could not. Instead, he pointed at the charts on the living room wall.

"You think you have it narrowed down?" Christine asked.

Arthur nodded. "We're getting closer to some definite possibilities."

"Are you going to tell Uncle Lane?"

Arthur went to the chart and pointed at an address. Christine stepped closer, looked at Arthur and saw the tears in his eyes.

"There's an anomaly here." He put his finger on the sketch of an apartment building. "I've collated all of the information from his various properties — there are over twenty of them. This one, this apartment building, isn't far from here. It's close to where Matt was taken. Down in the river valley, just next to the park and the river. The units on this floor all have lower power consumption than the units on the other floors." He glanced at another chart.

"Go on." Christine sat on the couch opposite the charts.

"Lori got us copies of the various power, gas and water readings from each of his properties. I was able to compare them to the norms. The energy company keeps track of those. They can tell when someone is likely to have a grow-op, for example. This apartment building has just the opposite problem. Too little consumption on this one floor." Arthur walked over to the phone. He picked it up. His eyes filled with tears and he took several long breaths. He handed the phone to Christine. "You tell him."

Christine stood up, took the phone and felt the weight of responsibility in her knees.

✕

"Lane here." He ducked his head as he looked for a clear spot through the river system of cracks in the Jeep's flat windshield so that he could see where they were going.

"Uncle Arthur thinks he knows where Matt is being held," Christine said.

"Where?" Lane looked across at Harper in the driver's seat.

"It's an apartment building on the south side of the river at one corner of the park. You know the one by the river? The one where we go to skate on the lagoon?" Christine asked.

Lane nodded. "Got you."

"Our best guess is that they're being held on the ninth floor. It appears that all the units on that floor are empty. We'd like you to take a look and see whether any of the units are being used now." Christine inhaled.

"We'll probably have to wait until it's dark and see whether any of the units have their lights on." Lane looked at Harper. "I'll call you back." Lane tapped the phone. "We're going to need a few things."

Harper listened and concentrated on keeping both eyes on Crowchild Trail as it curved around the naval reserve and descended into the river valley. A sandstone school was on their right. The road headed north and west toward the mountains.

"We need to hear from Saadiq's friend Hussein so we know who's doing the deliveries for Moreau. And we need to hear from Uncle Tran's cleaning connection. Then, if we still think we've got the location, we need McTavish to help us out." Lane looked down on the Bow River as they travelled over the bridge. He looked east where a kayaker paddled toward the Tenth Street Bridge.

"You sure we need McTavish?"

Lane rubbed the hair at the side of his head. "Yes. We can trust him to keep quiet, and he can get us the hardware we're going to need to make this work."

Jessica was crying. Matt wasn't sure for how long. Time was becoming elastic. He knew when it was night and when it was day because of the room's window. Besides that, he knew that morning brought the smell of coffee followed by the devil on the toilet.

"Shut her up!" the devil said.

"I'm trying." Matt rocked her and she looked up at him. He nodded at her. She continued to cry.

"Try harder!" The devil pounded on the door.

"Maybe a Popsicle will work," Matt said.

"Wuddya mean?" the devil asked.

"Popsicles. She loves those lemon ones from the super-market."

"Okay, I'll put an order in if she'll shut up!"

Matt smiled at Jessica, lifted his hand and closed the distance between his index finger and his thumb.

Jessica dropped the volume.

With Matt acting as her crying conductor, Jessica cried for another minute before she stopped and promptly pretended to fall asleep.

"Next time, we'll try for pizza," Matt whispered to her.

Jessica smiled as she snuggled up to Matt. "Then Daddy will find us." She crossed one ankle over the other. The red soles of her running shoes flashed once.

✕

They met McTavish for coffee and sandwiches at a café on Bowness Road. It was nearing dark — past the hour when joggers would stop to fuel and hydrate their toned bodies. The officers had the restaurant to themselves.

McTavish was dressed in casual clothes, as they were. His hair was greyer, but he still had a steady, focused presence.

"We're planning to hit the place if we get confirmation from one more source. And we need a favour." Lane took a mouthful of sandwich as his mind raced. *I've got to keep eating. This is my first food since breakfast.*

McTavish leaned a bit closer. His chair creaked. "Go on." He looked sideways at Harper.

Harper's right hand tapped the table. "We're waiting for some information on Moreau's drivers. He gets family members to do drug runs and deliveries for him. The kidnapper and our kids will need to eat. We also have a contact at a nearby restaurant. So, when the call comes, or we spot one of the delivery vehicles, we'll be in position to get the kids out. We're pretty certain about which floor they're on and we think we may know which room. We want to hit him when he's expecting someone else at the door."

"This whole business sounds a little iffy to me. I'm used to working with the TAC Unit. What exactly do you want me to do?" McTavish put his elbows on the table.

Lane said, "Right now we're working with the best information we have. Bringing in the TAC Unit would attract too much attention and probably warn the kidnappers. After the murder at Bearspaw Dam, we think we're running short on time. We're asking you to follow us in. Take the door in case we have any unexpected visitors."

McTavish nodded and leaned back. The chair creaked a warning.

For a moment Lane thought the chair would collapse.

McTavish apparently thought the same thing because he stood up, pulled another chair from a nearby table and sat in it. "That's better. You're also asking for some extra equipment, I think."

"We were hoping you could help us out in that department," Harper agreed.

"For hostage situations like this I like side arms and

shotguns. Automatic weapons tend to create a wider spread effect with their field of fire. I prefer the narrow spread provided by a close range shotgun blast or a Glock nine-millimetre." McTavish frowned.

"What?" Lane asked.

"We're talking about your kids, and I'm getting all technical on you. Making it sound too clinical. I'll take care of my end. Namely the weapons, ammunition and vests." McTavish reached for a sip of coffee. "Where and when do we meet?"

"Before we get to that, there's one other thing," Harper said.

"Harper and I leave with the kids before any other units show up. We're on leave so, technically, we shouldn't be there," Lane said.

"You don't want to lose the bust on a technicality but you want the kids out safe." McTavish looked out the window and onto the cul-de-sac.

"That's right. It's Moreau's building and his part of town. We have to expect some complications if we hang around for any longer than is absolutely necessary," Lane said.

McTavish turned back to face them and nodded. "Now, where do we meet when you get your confirmation?"

×

Robert Rowe heard his stomach grumble. He was in the city now and he'd found Centre Street. *All I have to do is walk south.*

He saw the school on his right. The chain-link fence came right up to the sidewalk. Traffic rushed by on his left.

He felt inside the pocket of the black leather jacket. His fingers touched the wooden handle of the dandelion weeder. Its forked tip was ready. He'd used a patch of concrete to sharpen the metal so that it would pierce flesh easily.

He breathed better when he was past the school and the

fence. Last night he'd had a nightmare about a schoolyard and Zander being chased. Robert was left to watch and feel that everlasting ache of helplessness as his brother was hunted down and killed by Moreau.

Robert reached an intersection and waited for the walk light. He looked down the hill and saw the Calgary Tower. *It still looks the same,* he thought, *but so much else has changed.* He remembered that the article said Kev's restaurant was almost in the shadow of the Calgary Tower. The walk sign blinked on. Robert crossed the street.

✕

Keely sat in her car and dialed.

"Arthur."

"It's Keely."

Arthur sat on the couch studying the charts and posters on the wall. On the coffee table in front of him there were markers, a yellow notepad, multicoloured sticky notes and a coffee cup. "What have you got?"

Daniel and Christine appeared in the doorway to the kitchen. "Who is it?" Christine asked.

Erinn sat up on the couch. "Well?"

Arthur covered his right ear with his hand, stared at the floor and listened.

"I've got a list for you. Got a pen and paper handy?" Keely asked.

Arthur reached for the pen and pad of yellow paper on the coffee table. "Go."

"Tell Lane that Hussein found five more vehicles, owner IDs and license plates for him. Here they are." Keely listed them. "I'm emailing Harper the photo IDs of the drivers so he and Lane will be able to identify them."

Arthur wrote down the information. "We're getting close."

"I sure hope so." Keely continued, "Still no luck locating

Mary Lowell. I've got three more shelters to visit tomorrow. Hope Moreau hasn't gotten to her first."

"Thanks."

"Anything new at your end?" Keely asked.

"I think we have a pretty good guess at the location where the kids are being held." Arthur looked at the others in the room awaiting an update.

"Good," Keely said.

"We think it's an apartment building." Arthur rubbed his eyes.

"With the vehicles and owners, Lane should be able to zero in on the apartment. I pity the poor bastard who's holding the kids after those two get hold of him," Keely said.

"You think it'll get worse?" Arthur asked.

"Only for Moreau and his mob. We'll track them all down after this." Keely hung up.

"Well?" Christine asked.

"We have more vehicle IDs and the owners. Now Lane and Harper will know exactly who to look for. That means we may know even more by tomorrow," Arthur said.

Erinn wrapped her arms tightly around her ribs. She shook her head.

Arthur stood.

Christine hugged Erinn.

"I don't know how you stay so calm," Erinn said.

"Simple," Christine said. "We all promise to fall apart when Jessica and Matt are home safe."

Robert walked past the wall of glass that allowed patrons to see out but made it difficult for passersby to see in.

He sat on a bench just east of Kev Moreau's restaurant.

Fifteen minutes later, Kev stepped out the front door and onto the mall. Moreau looked up at his sign. The neon light flickered. The name Kev went bright white, then off, only to warm up and flicker again.

Robert saw that Moreau was wearing clothes that fit him like they were made to make a statement, to draw attention.

Robert stood and felt for the weapon in his pocket.

Kev looked away from the sign and walked back into the restaurant.

Robert sat back down and considered his options.

He took a look at his clothes and had a quick sniff at his right armpit. "The front door won't work."

Robert stood and walked east. He counted doorways as he moved to the end of the block and turned left. Then he turned left at the alley. He counted doorways and followed his nose.

He stopped at a blue metal door close to a dumpster. *Kev's* was written in white paint on the blue. A black Mercedes was parked close to the wall.

Robert looked around him.

The back door to Kev's opened. A man in a black shirt and pants heaved two green garbage bags into the dumpster.

Robert waited for the door to close. He looked at the shadows creeping up the side of the brick building across the alley from Kev's. He walked up to the dumpster, got up on his toes, opened the fresh bags of garbage and began to graze.

×

Russell watched his crew put the finishing touches on cleanup. Grills gleamed after being scrubbed down, dishes were still hot to touch after being washed, dried and stacked, and the fridge was cooling what little food there was left. Aprons were tossed into the white bag for tomorrow's laundry pickup.

Russell waved at the sous-chef as he walked out the front door. Russell locked the glass door at top and bottom and then worked the deadbolt. For the last time, he wondered where Mary and Joshua were. "I hope she calls."

"You hope who calls?" Kev asked.

Russell looked to his right. Kev Moreau had the sleeves of his green tailor-made shirt rolled up. His jacket hung off the bar chair. In front of him were the receipts and cash for the night.

"Mary. I hope she calls." Russell saw the predatory look in Kev's eyes. Russell decided to change the subject. "It was a good night."

"Very good." Kev put the paper in the cashbox and locked it. "Wait a minute for me to put this in my office and I'll walk out the back with you."

Russell walked past the bar, into the kitchen and toward the back door. He watched as Moreau rolled down his sleeves, put on his jacket and checked his look in the mirror before closing and locking his office door.

"Remember, if Mary calls you, the next person you call is me." Moreau pointed at his chest.

Russell nodded as he set the alarm and reached for the back door.

"You and I have history. We look out for one another," Kev said.

Russell turned the deadbolt.

Moreau put his hand on Russell's shoulder. "I've always got your back. Remember that."

Russell turned the doorknob and caught the early-morning back alley stink of garbage left sitting too long in the summer's heat. He looked down the alley for his car.

Behind Russell, Moreau pushed the door shut and locked it. The light above the door carved a sharp half circle out of the night.

"I've been waiting a while." Robert stepped into the open from behind a telephone pole.

"Who are you?" Russell asked.

Moreau stood behind Russell.

"Zander's brother, Robert." He moved to the middle of the alley and faced Russell.

Russell saw a flashback of that day he handed Zander over to Moreau. Russell watched the boy get into Moreau's car. He saw Pike's smile and the frown on the face of Moreau's girlfriend. *What was her name?* Russell thought.

Moreau said, "I heard about you breaking out of Bowden."

"Just walked away after I heard the police found Zander's body." Robert had his right hand in the pocket of his jacket.

"I was really sorry to hear what happened to Zander," Moreau said.

Robert pulled the dandelion weeder from his jacket pocket. "You always were a fuckin' liar."

Russell felt a hand push him between the shoulder blades.

Robert bent his arm at the elbow. Metal flashed in the harsh clarity of the back alley light.

Russell put his arms forward. He found himself looking into the face of Robert Rowe, stinking of garlic and sweat. The forked end of the dandelion tool entered Russell's torso just below the ribs of his left side. He fell to his knees. His hands went to the wooden handle of the weapon.

There was the sound of feet running west along the alley.

Robert grunted as he worked to pull the dandelion weeder free. "Run, you bastard!"

Russell fell onto his back.

"Hold still!" Robert leaned over and pushed his left palm against Russell's chest, then pulled the weapon free.

Russell shuddered from the wrenching agony in his chest. He heard Robert's feet on pavement as he pounded after Moreau.

Russell looked up at the night sky. He could see one planet. He stared at the reflected light. He could hear Mary's voice saying, "There's the truth and being able to do something about it. Moreau has been pulling your strings for so long, you can't do a thing with what you know to be true. You know he killed Zander and you'll never do a thing about it!"

Russell's eyes lost the ability to focus.

chapter 13

Matt woke to the sound of the train grunting its way up the river valley. The locomotive was building up momentum to tackle the Rocky Mountains. Matt stood on the bed to look out of the window. *It must be late morning.*

Not much to see but tree tops and the other side of the valley. He sat down on his bed and looked over at Jessica.

Outside the door and down the hall, a phone rang.

Matt held his breath.

"Where's my coffee?" the devil asked.

Matt saw that Jessica had her thumb stuck in her mouth. There was a silver pool of drool on the pillow.

"Wuddya mean he's thinking about more insurance?" the devil asked.

Matt took a slow breath and sat down on the edge of the mattress.

"Look, if he's getting ready to do something else, he'd better let us know what's up. I'm not gonna hang around here much longer listening to that kid scream. . . . I don't care if Kev had a bad night. He needs to make up his mind!"

Matt heard the sound of plastic slammed against plastic.

He put his elbows on his knees and listened.

"Yes, I'd like to order some coffee. You know, the usual. Twenty minutes? Okay," the devil said.

Matt waited. He knocked on the door.

"What?"

"Bathroom," Matt said.

The devil smelled of sweat and day-old pizza as he opened the door. "Make it quick."

"Okay." Matt walked down the hall to the bathroom. He left the door open, dropped his pants and sat.

The devil watched him from the other end of the hall.

Matt glanced at the garbage can. Inside was a paper coffee cup with a cardboard heat sleeve. Matt leaned forward.

The devil faced away as he dialed and put the cordless phone to his ear.

Matt reached into the wastebasket, pulled out the empty cup, pulled off the sleeve and put the cup back in the trash.

"He always takes care of himself first. The plan is changing and I don't like it!" the devil said.

Matt stood up.

"If he says he's getting more insurance, it means he's about to cut us loose. Find out more! Kev will leave us to take care of these kids and take all of the heat from the cops!" The devil stabbed at a button on the phone.

Matt flushed the toilet, pulled up his pants, put the cardboard sleeve in the sink, washed his hands and rolled the cardboard into a wet ball. He squeezed the moisture out of the sleeve and palmed it.

He stepped outside the bathroom. "Finished."

"You know what to do." The devil pointed at the room with a doorknob on the outside but none on the inside.

Matt reached the door, opened it and used his thumb to jam the ball of cardboard into the mortise. Moisture trickled down the doorjamb. Matt smoothed the wet cardboard with his thumb. *I hope I got it right.* He closed the door. Jessica sat up in bed. He put his forefinger to his lips. She nodded.

He waited for the devil to twist the deadbolt. Instead, the man dialed another number. "I want to order a pizza."

✕

Arthur opened his eyes, took a sip of coffee and studied the charts on the wall, all tagged with multicoloured sticky notes.

He set the cup down on a coaster.

Christine was gently snoring where she lay on an air mattress to one side of the living room floor.

Roz lifted her head and wagged her tail.

Daniel appeared in the door to the kitchen. "Want another coffee?"

Arthur smiled. "Perfect."

"Anybody phone?" Erinn stood at the top of the stairs leading to the upstairs bedrooms. She was dressed in a red-flannel pajama top and matching bottoms. She held her belly as she felt her way down the steps.

"Not yet," Daniel said.

×

Mary wiped Joshua's face. He swung his head from side to side attempting to escape the facecloth.

"That's mean." Dee Dee entered the common room. "Let me take him for you." She reached out her arms.

"No, thanks." Mary tried to hide the anger in her voice as she stood and grabbed the empty baby bottle.

"Just trying to help." Dee Dee rolled her eyes. "New mothers."

"Give me a break! You call yourself a doula?" Mary took Joshua and headed for the back door. "See you next time."

"What did you say to me? I know what that means! How could you say that to me? I was trying to help!" Her shrill voice followed Mary down the hall.

Mary stepped out the back door. She looked at her son. *We need to get out of here.*

×

Lane closed his eyes and rubbed them with the back of his hand. He inhaled. *It's getting a little gamey in here.*

Harper shifted his position in the driver's seat. "Want a cup of coffee?"

"How long did I nod off?" Lane looked up at the ninth floor of Kev's apartment building nestled in the picturesque river valley. *I need a shower.*

"Thirty-five minutes." Harper pointed as a truck arrived at the front entrance of the apartment. He grabbed the binoculars. He focused on the driver and waited until he could see the rear license plate. "It's one of the trucks on the list. Let's see what he's delivering."

They watched as the driver parked, opened the door and stepped out holding a tray with a pair of coffees and a juice.

Lane looked at his watch.

A blue jay squawked from a nearby tree.

They ignored the bird.

The deliveryman stepped out of his truck, pushed open the front door and reached for a cell phone.

Lane checked his watch and wrote down the time, the license number and a description of the driver.

"Use the camera," Harper said.

Lane tapped the side of his head. "It's in here."

The deliveryman stepped out the front door three minutes later, pulled away from the apartment, ran the stop sign at the three-way intersection and turned left in front of them.

"What's the rush?" Harper asked.

"Don't know." Lane's phone rang and he reached for it. "Hello."

"It's Keely. I've got two more shelters to check on. Mary has to be at one of them. I'll let you know if I find her," she said.

"Do me a favour?" Lane asked.

"What's that?" she asked.

"Be sure to wear your vest. I can feel this thing rising up

to a boil and who knows which way it will go." Lane thought, *I could have explained it better.*

"You got yours on?" Keely asked.

"Yes," Lane said.

"Okay, then," Keely said. "I've got some news for you."

Lane leaned forward and glanced at Harper. "Go ahead."

"Russell Lowell is dead. Stabbed behind Kev's restaurant at about one o'clock this morning. Moreau is claiming that Robert Rowe was waiting at the back of the restaurant and is responsible for the murder." Keely waited for a reaction.

"If we're right, Rowe had a reason for coming after Moreau. But why would he want to hurt Russell Lowell?" Lane asked.

"Don't know. Details are sketchy so far," Keely said. "It's kind of ironic, though."

"How's that?' Lane asked.

"Kev was being interviewed on TV this morning. He was whining about the recent string of murders and complaining that the police aren't doing enough to protect citizens."

Lane said, "If things work out today, he may be complaining from a cell after being arrested for murder."

"Let's hope so." Keely hung up.

×

Mary sat under the apple tree in the shelter's backyard. Each time she looked up at the second floor of the shelter, the curtain to Dee Dee's window would shift to one side or the other.

"Don't pay no attention to her. She's here two or three times a year, and she always goes back to the bastard. Sometimes you just wanna shake your head. Thinks because she's a regular she has some kinda special status around here." Rita used her key to open the back gate. She carried a new shovel and digging fork. As the gate shut and locked behind her, she held the pair up. "Wore the other tools right out.

Got my first pension check, so I decided to treat myself."

Mary looked up at Dee Dee's window and saw the curtains move again. "Dee Dee gives me the creeps."

Rita stuck the spade in the soil and used the fork to turn over the dirt in the flowerbed. "I know. She pretends to be all nice and sweet, but underneath she's just plain mean. Loves to manipulate people around this place, then gets all offended when they won't play her games. She's one twisted woman. Keep on expecting to see her pop up on some reality show."

"You're starting to sound like a shrink." Mary put Joshua down on the grass. He crawled in the general direction of Rita, spotted a grasshopper and stopped to see whether he could grab it.

"When I worked for the city, people were always comin' to me for advice. Askin' me what they should do. Tellin' me their problems." Rita turned and smiled at Joshua. The grasshopper jumped. Joshua followed.

"I get the feeling it's time for me to move on." Mary glanced over her shoulder.

"Where you gonna go?" Rita asked.

"I don't know. That's the problem," Mary said.

"Family messed up?" Rita asked.

"Alcoholics." Mary watched her son like a mama grizzly bear watches over her cub.

"You want to protect him. That's natural," Rita said. Joshua reached for the grasshopper and it leapt away.

"You don't understand," Mary said.

Joshua began to chuckle. Rita smiled.

"Candace was there, wasn't she? When Moreau and Pike picked up Zander. Russell—my husband—told me there was a girl in the car. Russell still has nightmares about it. Pike conned Russell into bringing Zander to Moreau's car after school that day. Russell watched them drive away with the kid." Mary looked at the gate, then up at Dee Dee's window.

Except for Joshua's laughter and a robin, there was silence. Rita coughed. "Candace told me about it just before she left. She said they took Zander to an industrial park. Then Pike and Moreau took the kid inside a shop. About ten minutes later, they came out without the boy. Moreau told her, 'Don't worry, we're just teaching the kid's big brother a lesson. Zander is fine.' But after a couple of weeks, she knew Zander wasn't fine. She started to ask questions. A week after that, Pike showed the movie of her and Kev to kids at her school. She said Moreau and Pike showed it because she asked too many questions about Zander."

Mary heard the resignation in Rita's tone.

Rita said, "The thing is — you and I know what Kev is capable of. Most people don't. They buy his act. Neither of us falls for his charm. There's an advantage in that."

"Yes, but where's our advantage when he's got the gun?" Mary asked.

×

Matt touched Jessica's hand.

He pointed at her pink shoes with the flashing heels.

She walked over to the head of her mattress and brought her shoes to him.

From just outside of the door, the devil said, "I ordered that pizza you've been waitin' for. It's comin' for lunch. You hear me?"

"Thanks," Matt said. *Time for our last meal?* He heard the rustle of a newspaper and the footsteps of the devil walking down the hall. Matt bent to do up Jessica's right shoe. "Hold on to this one." He handed her the left shoe.

The bathroom fan turned on. Matt heard the sound of a belt buckle hitting the tile floor. He grabbed Jessica's hand. She dropped her left shoe.

Now! He put his free hand up and covered his mouth.

Jessica did the same. Matt reached his fingers under the door and pulled it toward him.

Jessica grabbed his wrist with both hands. The door swung open and the latch clicked. *Shit!* Matt thought when he heard the sound. He waited.

The devil turned the newspaper page and grunted.

Matt opened the door, picked Jessica up and swung around to close the door behind them. He looked down the hallway and saw the devil's knees with his pants around his ankles. The devil's hands were on either side of the newspaper. The rest of the devil was hidden behind the open door.

Matt tiptoed over to the apartment door, opened it, stepped through and set Jessica down. He used his hand to slow the closing of the door. He waited until he heard the latch make a whispered click. He bent, picked Jessica up under the armpits and walked down the hall. With every footstep he expected to hear the sound of a door opening and the devil's footsteps behind them.

Matt reached the stairwell door, pushed it open and let it close slowly. By the time they'd made their way down nine flights of stairs, his calves were burning, his arms were aching and his back was groaning.

The midday light greeted them as he opened the door to the main floor. He turned left, ignoring the front exit, turned the corner and opened the back door. He felt a rush of optimism when he inhaled fresh air.

Jessica asked, "Where's my daddy?" Matt followed a sidewalk that turned into a trail when it passed under the trees. He skidded on loose gravel where the trail curved its way down to join a paved path that followed the river. They went under the bridge with the river on their left. The sound of the water helped to calm him.

Jessica had her arms around his neck and whispered into his ear. "Where's my mum?"

Mary carried Joshua inside the shelter.

"You need to see this!" Dee Dee called out to Mary from the common room.

Mary looked at the TV. A reporter stood in front of Kev's restaurant. The reporter lifted his microphone. "Police discovered the body of Kev's chef Russell Lowell in the alley behind this restaurant just after two AM this morning." Mary felt as if she wanted to run but her feet kept her staked to the floor.

The reporter continued. "Kev Moreau is the owner of the restaurant."

The image switched to Kev Moreau facing the camera. "Russell was a long-time employee. I tried to get between him and Rowe, but it all happened so fast."

The reporter asked, "So you witnessed the murder?"

Moreau nodded. "It happened right in front of me. Rowe stabbed Russell before I could intervene. How could the prison system let a guy like Rowe just walk away from jail? Makes me wonder who will protect any honest citizen from people convicted of violent crimes."

Mary felt the tears running down her cheeks. She felt Joshua's hand on her arm. *Kev is lying!* She looked at Dee Dee.

She saw the smile on Dee Dee's lips.

Mary turned away and walked toward the stairs. *Russell, I tried to tell you.*

Lane reached for his phone. "Yes?"

"It's Arthur. Uncle Tran's friend got an order for the pizza we've been waiting on. The phone number is a match for one of Moreau's drivers. The pizza will be picked up in twenty minutes," Arthur said.

"We're ready."

"Lane?" Arthur asked.

"I know. I'll call you as soon as I know. Right now I'm trying to concentrate and make sure we're ready." Lane tucked the phone in his pocket. He looked at Harper. "We're on in less than thirty." Lane dialed McTavish's number.

×

There was a gentle knock on Mary's door.

Mary picked Joshua up and held him close. "Who is it?"

"Rita."

Mary opened the door. Joshua stuck his tongue out.

Rita tried to smile. "I was just downstairs and overheard Dee Dee on the phone. She clammed up tight when I walked into the common room. You two had better come home to stay with me for a few days."

Mary began to decline, then looked at her son. "When do you want to leave?"

"Meet me at the back gate in fifteen minutes." Rita reached for the doorknob.

"Russell is dead. He was killed this morning," Mary said.

"All the more reason for you to leave." Rita closed the door.

×

Kev Moreau tapped the sous-chef on the back as he prepared vegetables for the lunch crowd. "I'll be back soon. I'm leaving you in charge, chef."

The newly promoted chef beamed at Moreau.

Moreau smiled back. "You'll be just fine. I have every confidence in you. I have something that needs to be taken care of right away." He pulled his car keys out of his pocket as he walked out the back door.

×

Keely stopped at a red light. She looked at the address of the last shelter on her list. The light turned green. She headed west along the north side of the river across from the towers of the downtown core.

✕

Matt carried Jessica under the bridge. He heard traffic humming overhead. In front of them, a paved path headed east into a park where trees and shrubs would hide them.

"We have to go this way, Jess," Matt said.

Jessica had one arm around his neck. "Home?"

"Yes, we're going home." Matt followed the trail deeper into the cover. He remembered a series of pedestrian bridges that connected the south side of the river with the north. "This way might take us a little while longer, but it will be harder for anyone to find us. Can you walk?"

Jessica released his neck. He put her on the ground. She was unsteady on her feet.

"Feels funny to walk after being in that tiny room for so long."

Jessica walked ahead of him. Her single heel flashed red.

"We forgot one of your shoes." Matt looked down the trail. *We need to put some distance between us and the devil!*

✕

Lane and Harper had walked over to wait in the apartment foyer. Moreau's relative drove up in his late-model Ford pickup. He stepped out of the truck with a pizza in one hand and a cigarette in the other. He looked to be about thirty and weighed maybe one hundred fifty pounds. The man wore a red-and-white hockey jersey and a red ball cap. The information supplied by Saadiq's friend told them that this cousin went by the name of Billy Moreau. He left the diesel engine of his pickup idling.

McTavish stepped out from cover. He leveled a shotgun at the man's nose. "Put the pizza on the hood, Billy."

"Do you know who you're messing with?" Billy's cigarette fell from his mouth and rolled under the truck.

"Billy Moreau. Cousin to Kevin Moreau." McTavish held out his police ID.

Billy put the pizza on the hood of the truck.

"Move to the front of your truck and put your hands on the hood," McTavish said.

"Yep." Billy made to inhale on his cigarette, frowned when he discovered it was gone, stepped over to the front of the Ford and leaned with both hands on the chromed brush guard.

McTavish placed the barrel of his shotgun on the collar of Billy's jersey and pressed the metal up against the back of his neck.

"I just do what I'm told," Billy said.

McTavish used his free hand to check Billy for weapons. The officer found a cell phone in Billy's right pants pocket.

"That's my phone, man!"

"You've got other problems now. Unlawful confinement is one of them. I'm going to detain you." McTavish pocketed the phone and reached for handcuffs. He attached one end of the handcuffs to the truck's brush guard and the other to Billy's right wrist. Then he stood back and faced Moreau.

"What do you say to him when you deliver the pizza?" McTavish asked.

"Nuthin'," Billy said.

"I'm only going to ask once more," McTavish pointed the shotgun at the pavement.

"Nuthin'! I told you, nuthin'! Just knock once and go easy, man, he's my brother," Billy said.

"What's his name?"

"His name is Daryl. The kids are fine. No reason to hurt anyone," Billy said.

McTavish walked to the driver's door of the truck, reached inside, shut off the engine, pocketed the keys and asked, "What room number?"

Billy said, "Nine oh five."

McTavish looked at Billy and put his forefinger to his lips.

Billy nodded. "Yep. I'll keep my mouth shut. Just don't shoot my brother."

McTavish pushed the door of the lobby open and handed the pizza box to Lane.

Harper pressed the button for the elevator. The white arrow lit up. The elevator door slid open.

McTavish pulled a phone out of his pocket as he stepped inside the elevator. "The clock is ticking. I'm calling for backup."

×

Keely found the women's shelter two blocks back from a bluff overlooking downtown. She parked across the street and stared at the white two-storey building with its two-metre-high hedge shielding the grounds from prying eyes. It was flanked by one mansion made of red brick and another of sandstone.

She put her keys into her pocket, stepped out of the Chev and crossed the street. Keely looked at the trellis flowers visible over top of the hedge marking the front gate to the shelter. The hedge was manicured into an arch. Inside the yard, a woman gathered a shovel and garden tools from the far corner of the yard. She placed them in a wheelbarrow.

Another woman, with a bruised face, opened the front gate and smiled in Keely's direction.

Keely heard a car door close to her right. She walked between two parked cars and stepped onto the sidewalk. What she saw next became a series of impressions accompanied by her instinctive reactions.

She saw that Kev Moreau had a handgun pointed at her. Keely reached for the Glock on her hip.

Moreau smiled with an expression that said she was too late.

Keely reacted by diving back between the parked cars.

Moreau's silenced gun spat one round.

She heard it whiz past her left ear. The second round struck her in the left breast. She screamed in pain at the impact. Her head caught the corner of the car's grille. She smelled antifreeze and blood as she fell under the front bumper of the parked car.

Moreau looked down on the officer and saw the blood pooling around her head. He turned to walk through the gate. Dee Dee held the gate open for him. "She's around back with the kid."

×

"Puppy." Jessica pointed at a red animal walking across the near end of a pedestrian bridge crossing the Bow River.

Matt picked her up. "Fox."

The fox yawned and turned west as it stepped off the bridge and disappeared into the undergrowth.

"Mine?" Jessica pointed at the fox logo on her running shoe.

"That's right." Matt carried her onto the bridge and over the river to the north bank.

"Mommy's be mad." Jessica held up her toe and sock as proof.

Matt looked at the pink sock and its dirty sole. He smiled. "No, your mom won't be mad you lost your shoe. She'll be too happy to see you again."

"Promise?" Jessica said and put her left hand on his shoulder as she held on to his shirt front with the right.

"Promise."

×

McTavish pointed and indicated that Harper and Lane should stand on either side of the door. He handed the shotgun to Harper.

Lane held the pizza between McTavish and the door, just above the doorknob.

McTavish drew his Glock with his right hand and knocked once on the door with his left. He tucked his gun under the pizza box.

They heard a chair being pushed back.

A pair of boots crossed the floor.

"Billy?" asked the voice on the inside.

"Yep," McTavish said.

The door opened.

Daryl looked at the pizza. He raised his eyes. They opened wide and he reached for the weapon on his hip. His eyes crossed when he saw McTavish's left fist connect with his nose.

Daryl stumbled back and cupped his hands over his bloody nose.

Lane tossed the pizza against the opposite wall and stepped inside. The rage he had contained for the past days exploded as he grabbed Daryl by the hair, kicked the feet out from under him, twisted him in mid-air and dropped him face first onto the floor. Lane landed on top of Daryl with a knee in his back. Air whooshed out of Daryl's lungs.

By the time Harper stepped into the room, Daryl had both hands cuffed behind his back. He was taking in big gasps of air, coughing and spitting blood. After a minute, he asked, "What the fuck? You broke my nose!" Harper put a black nylon bag over Daryl's head.

McTavish grabbed the suspect by the arm, lifted the devil's pistol out of its holster and propped Daryl up against the wall where his nose could bleed onto the front of his black T-shirt. McTavish walked down the hall and checked the bathroom.

Lane drew his Glock and held it at his side. He held his finger lengthwise over the guard.

Harper closed the door to the apartment.

Lane looked at the kitchen table and saw Matt's phone. He reached for it.

Harper stopped him with his left hand. He shook his head. Harper pointed at the devil's mask near the remote control on the coffee table. He held up his left palm. He mouthed the words, *We're not here.*

McTavish reached the bedroom door, tried the handle and then raised his shoe and kicked the door open. It flew against the wall, smashed back against the casing and opened about halfway.

McTavish looked inside of the room, then over his shoulder. They could read the puzzlement in his eyes.

Harper leaned his head to the left.

Lane went to stand behind McTavish, who stepped inside the bedroom.

Inside the room was one mattress with two pillows on the floor. Next to the mattress, a pink running shoe lay on its side.

McTavish asked, "What is this child's running shoe doing here?"

The door opened too easily, Lane thought. He looked at the casing and spotted something jammed in the mortise. He pointed at it.

McTavish leaned to take a closer look. Then he looked at Lane and frowned.

Harper looked at them and opened his left hand as if to ask, *What's going on?*

McTavish put his finger to his lips. He held up the running shoe to make sure that Harper could see it.

Harper blanched and nodded.

McTavish said, "The place is empty except for you, Daryl." With his free hand, he motioned that Harper and Lane should wait in the living room.

Lane resisted an impulse to kick Daryl in the ribs as he walked past.

Harper cocked his right leg to kick Daryl. Lane shoved Harper, who stumbled into the living room. Daryl sniffed.

McTavish tried the door of the next bedroom. He opened the door and looked inside. He waved at Lane and Harper to come and take a look.

Another mattress was close to the door. The rest of the room was stacked floor to ceiling with cardboard boxes. McTavish hauled one down and opened it. He held up a wad of cash and waved it. "Room is filled with boxes." He lifted his chin and indicated they should leave the apartment.

Lane and Harper went outside and down the hallway. Harper asked, "What did you see?"

"The bedroom's empty. You saw Jessica's pink running shoe. It was on the floor. It looks like Matt's phone on the table. And there's something jammed in the mortise so the door wouldn't lock." Lane leaned against the wall. "I don't know where Matt and Jessica are."

Harper put his free hand on Lane's shoulder.

McTavish opened the apartment door while keeping his gun trained on Daryl. The sergeant said, "He says he doesn't know where the kids are. Said the kids were there this morning. Seemed real surprised the room was empty." With his free hand, McTavish reached for his phone and pressed speed dial. "With all of the cash in that room, this place is going to be real busy, real soon." He lifted his chin to indicate that they should leave, then spoke into his phone. "Hello. It's McTavish. I need the Forensic Crime Unit."

✕

"Arthur? It's me." Lane thought, *What do I say to him?*

"What's the matter?" Arthur asked.

"I . . ." Lane followed Harper across the street as they headed back to the Jeep.

"What? Tell me!" Arthur said.

"They weren't there. Matt's phone was there. Jessica's running shoe was there. Someone had jammed something in their door to keep it from locking. The guy who was guarding them was surprised the kids weren't in the room. I don't know where they are right now!" *I can't think,* Lane thought. *I need to think and I can't!*

"Pull it together, Detective," Arthur said.

Lane was sure there was a smile behind Arthur's voice. Lane thought, *What's the matter with him?*

"What does the evidence tell you, Detective?" Arthur asked.

"They escaped?" Lane opened the passenger door and climbed into the Jeep.

"You bet they did."

Harper started the Jeep. "Of course they escaped. Matt jammed something into the lock and walked them both outta there. Now, where did they go?"

×

Mary had Joshua snugged on her right hip and two plastic shopping bags in her left hand. She put the bags down to open the back gate.

"There you are," Kev Moreau said.

Mary recognized the voice and reached for the gate latch.

"I wouldn't do that."

Mary turned and held Joshua close to her side.

Kev stood on the back door step. Dee Dee stood behind him.

"I'm leaving this place. You have nothing to fear from me," Mary said.

Kev stepped down and stood on the lawn with his hands on his hips. Dee Dee remained on the steps with her arms crossed under her breasts. She was smiling.

Kev held his hands open.

Mary saw the gun in its holster under his left arm.

"It's not that easy. Things got complicated after you killed Pike." Kev took one step closer.

"He was going to take Joshua. Just like the two of you took Zander." Mary saw Rita walking down the side of the house with the shovel in her right hand. Moreau had his back to Rita.

Kev drew his gun and pointed it in Mary's direction. "See what I mean about things being complicated?"

"Yes, that means I get a two-bedroom apartment instead of one," Dee Dee said.

Kev turned and fired.

A red mark appeared on Dee Dee's forehead, and she took a step back.

Kev shot her in the heart.

Dee Dee bent at the knees and fell sideways into a shrub.

Kev turned to face Mary. "Put the boy down on the grass. If you hadn't told me what you know about Zander, I might have let you walk."

Mary moved to her right and sat Joshua down on the grass. She retreated from her son. "How did Russ die?"

"He got in the way of Rowe's knife," Kev said.

"So, you used him as a shield." Mary watched as Rita moved closer to Moreau.

"That's why this needs to be done. You know too much and ask too many questions. Women like you always ask too many questions." Kev raised his pistol.

A whistle of steel cut through air. Kev started to turn his head. He heard a moist thunk as the shovel blade chopped through flesh and bone. Kev's head flicked to the right.

Mary stared at Moreau.

His face paled. The gun dropped from his useless right hand. He reached over with his left hand, trying to pull at the shovel blade embedded between his neck and shoulder. "Wait a minute," he said to Mary. "Just wait there." His right hand flopped and swung uselessly at his side. He turned to face Rita, who had picked up his gun and was pointing it in his general direction.

"I'll take that." He took a step toward her.

Rita stepped to her right.

Moreau stumbled forward, turned to follow her and — as he did so — continued to pull at the shovel with his left hand. "Why did you do that?"

Mary wondered at the offended bewilderment in Kev's voice.

He dropped to his knees. "I don't even know who you are."

Rita leveled the gun at Moreau's face. "I'm Candace Barnett's aunt."

"Candy's aunt. How is Candy?" Moreau put his left hand out to keep himself from falling sideways.

"Haven't seen her in years," Rita said. "She was another woman who asked too many questions, remember?"

Mary saw that Joshua had spotted a dandelion and was crawling toward it. She went to pick him up.

"What did you hit me with?" Moreau asked.

"A shovel." Rita kept the gun aimed at his eyes.

"You've got to be joking." Then he did something that left both women looking at each other with bewilderment.

He began to laugh.

The Jeep rolled out of the valley.

Harper's phone rang. He pulled it out of his pocket and handed it to Lane.

"Lane here."

"Simpson. We have a report that Detective Saliba has been shot and is requesting assistance. Will you two move on it?" he asked.

"What's the location?" Lane asked. *How did he get this number?*

Simpson read the address to Lane, who relayed it to Harper.

Harper turned onto Crowchild Trail and accelerated.

What the hell happened to Keely?

✕

Arthur wrote the grocery list for Daniel and pushed a credit card across the table with his free hand. "Take this."

Daniel took the card. "I'll take my phone just in case you think of anything else."

"You go with him." Arthur pointed at Christine.

"But we don't know where they are," Christine said.

"We do know where they'll be headed. They were being held maybe five kilometres from here," Arthur said. "And I know when they get here we're all going to need something to eat."

"Go on, we'll be here." Erinn looked at Arthur with a mixture of hope and dread.

✕

Matt sat Jessica down on a bench toward the top end of the paved pathway leading up out of the river valley. He sat down beside her and looked further up the path where it wound its way into an established neighbourhood. Mature trees on either side of the path provided shade and cover.

They sat and watched a pair of boys race down the hill on their bicycles.

"I'm tired." Jessica held up one dirty-socked foot, rested it on Matt's leg and brought up the other foot with its pink running shoe. She rested her head on the back of the bench.

"Me too," Matt said.

"I want to go home."

"Me too. So, let's get going."

Jessica reached up, and he lifted her onto his shoulders.

✕

Mary looked at the scene from the back of a police cruiser. Joshua slept beside her on the seat. She kept one hand on his head.

Mary could see the back of Rita's head as she sat in a cruiser further down the street.

A Jeep pulled up and parked next to her. Two men got out and ran toward a woman on a stretcher, who was being loaded into an ambulance.

✕

Lane found Keely on the stretcher in the back of the ambulance. "What happened?"

Keely tried to lift her head. It was wrapped in white gauze. Her face was streaked with blood and tufts of her red hair were matted with it.

The EMT — whom Lane knew to be the mother of three — put her hand on Keely's shoulder to keep her horizontal.

"This is ridiculous. I was wearing a fucking vest!" Keely said.

Lane climbed into the back of the ambulance while the EMT put an oxygen mask over Keely's mouth.

Keely pulled the mask off. "They said some woman killed Moreau?"

"With what?" Lane asked.

"A shovel," the EMT said.

"Are you kidding me?" Keely asked. "I want to meet this woman. I mean, after the bastard shot me, the least I could do is thank her."

The EMT shook her head. "You can thank her later. We're taking you to the hospital. The bullet hit your vest very near your heart. You need to see a doctor. Besides, that scalp wound will need stitches."

"It didn't hit my heart, it hit my boob!" Keely rubbed her breast. "Shit, that hurt!"

The EMT looked at Lane.

"Better get her to the hospital," Lane said.

"Can't be soon enough." The EMT smiled.

Lane backed out of the ambulance and into Harper.

"She okay?" he asked.

Lane nodded. "Yes. I think she's at the tail end of an adrenalin rush. What happened back there?"

Harper looked at the open front gate of the women's shelter. "Two bodies in the backyard. One of them is Moreau. Face down in the grass. Looks like someone buried a shovel in his shoulder or his neck — hard to say which. The other body is an unidentified female. Fibre is on his way."

"Hey! Shut the doors, will you?" The EMT sat down next to Keely.

Lane grabbed one door and Harper the other. They closed and locked the back doors of the ambulance.

The ambulance's lights came on and it slalomed around the police cruisers and their flashing lights.

"Keely's okay." Lane looked at Harper.

"You said that. Now we have to find Matt and Jessica. Where the hell would they go?"

Lane looked at the ground and tried to think.

"You're always telling me that you like to walk the dog in that part of town. Where the hell would you go? You're the fucking detective," Harper said.

Lane thought for a moment. "There's a trail that runs up the north side of the river valley. Come on! Are you going to drive or stand around asking me questions?"

Jessica locked her fingers at the base of Matt's throat. He carried her piggyback while he walked over the bridge crossing Crowchild Trail.

Matt looked ahead.

"Are we there yet?" Jessica asked.

"Another half an hour."

"My arms are tired." Jessica tucked her head against his shoulder.

×

Harper drove the Jeep up the pathway on the north side of the river.

An approaching cyclist came around the corner and was forced onto the grass. His mouth formed a curse that became unintelligible as he bumped over the uneven surface and past the Jeep.

"What happens if we don't find them here?" Harper asked.

"Then we head back to the river and work our way west." Lane pointed ahead.

A woman — pushing a stroller almost as wide as the Jeep — shoved her child off to the side of the trail and shouted, "Motherfuckers!"

"Friendly bunch," Harper said. "These are your neighbours?"

×

Robert Rowe rested his elbows on the concrete wall of the pedestrian bridge running between Edworthy Park and the north side of the river. He stood between two circles in the cement. Each circle was inlaid with parallel lines of wire. Below him, the Bow River ran east. He spotted the shadow of a trout idling behind a rock. The green water swirled over the rock, creating a wave but no white water. The trout swam lazily, waiting for food to become trapped in the reverse current created by the rock and the river's flow. Robert backed up to look at the trout through the wire. He smiled at the thought of eating the fish.

A woman walked down the middle of the bridge. She saw the blood on Robert's shoes and walked a little faster. When she reached her car, she pulled a phone from her purse and dialed 911.

Fifteen minutes later, a police cruiser arrived in the parking lot on the south side of the river. They parked in the Edworthy Park lot, walked past the cooking shelter, paralleled the river and then walked up the sloped southern end of the bridge. Both officers were over six feet tall and each weighed more than two hundred pounds.

Robert focused on the trout and wondered whether he could wade into the water to catch it. "It looks to be at least two pounds."

The officers looked at one another. "He matches the description," one said.

"Robert Rowe?" the other officer asked.

Robert turned to face the officers.

The officers noticed the blood on the front of his shirt and down the front of his pants. The officers separated, keeping a distance of about two metres between them.

Robert reached into his pocket.

"Put your hands up and keep them away from your body!" Both officers put their hands on their Glock handguns.

Robert lifted the dandelion weeder out of his pocket. He held it out front with his right hand and pointed the weapon at the officers.

A cyclist rang his bell, rode between the officers, stood up on his pedals, passed Robert and accelerated.

One of the officers spoke into his radio.

"I didn't kill anyone that night. I was a passenger when those guys shot Moreau's cousin. I didn't know where they were driving or that they had guns until after I got in the car. But I was the one person someone recognized from that night. And that's why Zander died." Robert made eye contact with each officer in turn. "My brother died for no good reason."

"Drop the weapon." The officer looked to his right. Cyclists and pedestrians were gathering at the south end of the bridge. He looked to the north. More people were gathered at that end.

Robert looked at the dandelion weeder. "Killing that guy last night was an accident. I was after Kev Moreau."

"Moreau is dead," the second officer said.

Robert looked at the officers. "Somebody else killed him?"

The officer nodded. "That's correct. Now put the weapon down."

"It's a dandelion weeder." Robert stared at the blood he hadn't managed to wipe from the metal.

A siren sounded on the north side of the river. Robert looked north and focused on the concrete circles at that end of the bridge.

Another cyclist rode between the officers. This cyclist looked at Robert and said, "Fuckin' loser!" Then the rider spat on Robert.

Rowe swiped the dandelion weeder in a wide arc and caught the cyclist on the thigh. The rider screamed, lost control of his bike, fell and slid into the opposite wall.

Robert lunged at the cyclist.

One officer shouted, "Stop!"

The other fired two rounds.

Robert dropped the dandelion weeder, looked at the hole in his chest, looked through the circles at the north end of the bridge, stepped back toward the circle in the wall, sat down and looked down through the mesh to see whether he could spot the trout behind the rock.

×

"Here, you chop the celery." Arthur handed a knife and cutting board to Erinn.

"Thank you," Erinn said, hugged him and kissed him on the cheek.

Arthur said, "We have to keep busy. We'll get news soon. I just can't sit and wait anymore."

Someone knocked on the front door. Arthur and Erinn raced for it.

Maria stood on the doorstep with a fresh-baked pizza. "Hungry?"

×

At the top entrance to the trail, a vertical white metal pole blocked Harper's path.

"What do we do?" Lane asked.

Harper stopped, shifted the Jeep into low and moved ahead slowly. He smiled at Lane. When the Jeep's bumper met the pole, it fell over onto the pavement.

×

Matt's legs ached. His back ached. His feet ached. He felt wonderful and free. "Not much further."

He looked to his left. A pair of kits played tag above the sandstone rocks on the first level of the retaining wall. Matt looked for the mother but couldn't spot her. He heard the sound of an approaching car and the sound of brakes being applied hard. Matt looked over his shoulder. He swung Jessica off of his back, tucked her on his hip and made ready to run.

"Matt!" Christine was halfway out of the passenger window. When Daniel got the car stopped, she had some trouble getting back inside because she'd opened the door before releasing her seat belt.

Matt set Jessica on her feet.

Christine jumped from the car. She ran, grabbed Matt around the neck and kissed his cheek. "Matt!" Then she recoiled. "You stink!"

"Me too?" Jessica held her arms up.

Five minutes later, Jessica stepped in the back door carrying a bag of groceries. "Christine told me to bring these." She held up the bag.

Erinn turned, saw her daughter, blinked and scooped up her child.

"Mommy! You're squishing me!" Jessica said.

Lane's phone rang as they rolled along a trail set in between condos and an open field. "Yes?"

"They had to have gotten at least this far," Harper turned left into a parking lot and searched the area systematically with his eyes.

"They're home," Lane said.

"Home?" Harper turned to stare at Lane.

Lane nodded. "Christine and Daniel found them within a kilometre of my house. We're supposed to go there and have something to eat."

"You're kidding." Harper's eyes filled with tears. He stopped the Jeep, leaned against the wheel and wept.

Lane rubbed his friend's back with his left hand. "No, I'm not kidding. They're home."

chapter 14

"How are you feeling today?" Lane looked around the hospital room. Amir, Saadiq, Katherine and Dylan were like statues taking up four corners in Keely's room.

Keely rolled her eyes. "The doctor says I might get out today. He's being cautious about swelling around the heart. Moreau was a good shot." She shifted her weight and grimaced with pain. "But not quite good enough."

Amir, Keely's father, glared at Lane.

Saadiq, Keely's brother, moved toward Lane and embraced the detective. "Thank you for making her wear her vest."

"You did that?" Katherine, Keely's mother, asked.

"He did," Keely said.

Lane found himself at the centre of a group hug, communal weeping and even a kiss or three on his cheeks. He was left to wonder who was doing the kissing. When he was free and clear, he saw tears in Keely's eyes. He looked at Katherine and the portly Amir and said. "Saadiq showed us where to look for Matt and Jessica. We wouldn't have found them without your daughter and your son."

"How are Matt and Jessica doing?" Dylan asked.

"They're both downstairs being checked out. It's a precaution. Someone turned Jessica's motor on. She won't stop talking or moving, and her mother and father won't let her out of their sight. They're getting plenty of exercise and can't wipe the smiles off their faces. I'm afraid Erinn will go into labour if Jessica doesn't slow down soon." Lane reached into his pocket, pulled out a gift card and handed it to Keely.

"Thought you might want some new tunes to listen to while you're recuperating."

Keely took the certificate and smiled. "Think my old stuff is that bad?"

Lane shook his head. "No."

Katherine said, "We're going for dinner when she gets out. Would your family like to come?"

"Of course," Lane said.

"What about Mary? What's happened to her?" Keely asked.

"She's thinking about selling her house and moving. And Simpson called. He wants the two of us to do her interview," Lane said.

"What happened out back of the women's shelter? No one told me very much." Keely sat up and winced.

Lane looked around the room.

Katherine said, "Come on, we've got to get something to eat while these two talk shop."

The room emptied and the door closed.

Lane said, "Things were kind of tense in here."

"You think?" Keely smiled. "At least everyone is in the same room. My dad is pissed off because I won't be an obedient little girl. Nothing new there. Come on, tell me what happened."

"According to Fibre's initial findings, the deceased woman was killed by two shots from Moreau's Smith and Wesson. Moreau died from massive hemorrhaging due to the wound inflicted by the shovel blade. Mary and her baby are fine. A woman named Rita — who volunteered at the shelter — has admitted to swinging the shovel. Rita and Mary are the people we need to interview. When would you like to do that?" Lane watched Keely cup her left breast as she coughed.

"How about tomorrow?" Keely asked.

"But you're not even out of the hospital yet," Lane said.

Keely glared at him. "I'm not going to spend another day like today with those four watching over me. I feel like I've just been kicked out of Sunday school again by the Imam."

"You got kicked out of Sunday school?" Lane asked.

"More than once," Keely said.

"How come?"

"I asked too many questions. I have been a constant source of embarrassment to my father." Keely swung her legs over the side of the bed. "Hand me that housecoat, will you?"

"Are you supposed to get up?" Lane handed her the robe.

Keely shrugged. "I'm tired of doing what I'm told. Besides, I want to see that Matt and Jessica are fine. You're taking me down to visit them." She smiled as he held the robe open for her. "How bad is my hair?" She breathed into her fist. "And my breath?"

"I'll keep away," Lane said.

"And I have to talk with you. My RCMP boss says my time with the city police is up. They want me to transfer to Central Canada. It seems that female officers who speak Arabic are in demand." She waited for Lane to reply.

"I don't know what to say." Lane helped her into the robe. *I feel like I've been punched in the belly.*

"Besides, it would be good for Dylan and me to live away from my father."

Lane frowned and looked to see that the door was closed. "You're probably right about that."

chapter 15

Three women, one baby and a lawyer sat across the table from Lane and Keely. The lawyer insisted the detectives meet around a table at the lawyer's downtown office.

"We have some information on the deaths of Stan Pike and Kevin Moreau. What we'd like to do is gather as much additional information as possible to determine where to proceed from here," Lane said.

Keely shifted in her seat, leaned back and tried to get comfortable.

The woman sitting next to the lawyer was about thirty but had the eyes of someone much older despite her long blonde hair.

She could have been a model if she was interested in that kind of life, Lane thought.

The woman turned to face Keely. "Can I take a look at your wound?"

"Who are you?" Keely asked.

"Candace Barnett." She pointed at Rita. "She's my aunt."

"What's your interest in what happened to me?" Keely asked.

"Professional. I work for MSF," Candace said.

"MSF?" Keely asked

"*Médecins sans frontières*. I often see gunshot wounds. I just wonder what one looks like when a vest stops a bullet." Candace kept her tone neutral.

She paid for the lawyer and now she's trying to gain a little trust with a 'sister', Lane thought.

"You a doctor?" Keely pushed her chair back and stood up.

"Nurse." Candace got up and walked around the table.

Keely turned her back to Lane. He turned to watch the lawyer. The lawyer stopped smiling when she saw the detective watching her. The lawyer, Ms. Scott, had short blonde hair and wore a white blouse, black slacks and a tailored black jacket.

Candace pointed at the stitches on Keely's forehead. "Moreau went for the head shot?"

"I heard a bullet go past my ear," Keely said.

Lane turned to watch the show.

Candace leaned to take a close look at Keely's breast. "And then he went for the heart shot."

"We figure that Pike and Moreau were involved in a series of murders, including Zander, of course. I guess you heard about Roberta King?" Keely asked.

Nice work, Keely. Let her know you won't be played, Lane thought.

"No, I haven't heard. What happened to Ms. King?"

"Someone poured gasoline around her house and set fire to it. She died in the fire," Lane said.

"That's a shame. It doesn't surprise me, though. And you can't be so naïve as to think they haven't killed a few more people over the past ten years. I mean, for a few years you must have suspected them for any number of drive-by shootings as they established their territory and then consolidated it." Candace stood up straight. "Be careful with that. The bruising looks pretty deep."

"That's what my doctor told me after he put me on blood thinners." Keely buttoned up her blouse, turned around and sat down.

Candace walked back around the table. Her hand brushed Rita's shoulder as she passed.

"Can we get down to business?" Keely asked.

Candace frowned. "I was in the car when Pike and Kev

picked up Zander. They said they were trying to teach his big brother a lesson. Robert Rowe was Zander's older brother. He and Kev had a falling out. Robert was a passenger during a drive-by where one of Kev's cousins was killed."

"You know where they took Zander?" Lane asked.

"It was a shop in an industrial park. I think Moreau's grandfather owned it at the time. Kev said they were going to leave Zander there overnight as a warning to Robert. But that's not what happened, obviously." Candace looked at her aunt.

"When did you know that they'd killed Zander?" Keely asked.

"I didn't know for sure until I got a call from my mother telling me that his body was found. Then I got another call explaining that Aunt Rita was in trouble. I did start asking questions about a week after they took Zander. But Kev and Pike, well, they had ways of getting people to shut up." She turned her focus to Lane. "You know all about it." She looked at Rita. "My aunt knows all about it. You either played along with Kev or he made you pay."

"Where were you three days ago?" Keely asked.

"Africa," Candace said.

"Why are you here now?" Lane asked.

"I heard about what happened. It was time for me to come back and tell what I know. What I saw. To put what Rita and Mary did into some kind of context. If you know what happened to Zander, then you know why Mary did what she did. And you know why my Aunt Rita did what she did." Candace put her palms down on the table.

"Mary?" Lane waited for eye contact before he asked, "What was Pike doing at your house the day he died?"

Mary lifted her head. Joshua stuck a plastic toy in his mouth. A pool of drool appeared on the front of his red T-shirt. "He came to the door and said he was taking Joshua away. I tried to stop him. He hit me in the face and went upstairs. When he came back down with Joshua, I had a knife. Pike was holding Joshua out like a shield, so I aimed for Pike's crotch."

"Anything happen after that?" Keely asked.

"I took Joshua and walked away. Caught a bus and asked the driver where the women's shelter was. That's where I met Rita," Mary said. Joshua pulled the toy out of his mouth. A thread of drool connected boy and toy.

Rita looked around the table.

"Go ahead," Candace said.

"About six months after I retired from drivin' bus for the city, I came to volunteer at the shelter in my neighbourhood." Rita saw Lane's frown and said, "You're wonderin' how I could afford to live in such an expensive neighbourhood aren't you?"

Lane nodded. *She's quick.*

"Moved there twenty-five years ago. Wasn't such a trendy place then. Anyway, I saw what Candy had done with her nursing with MSF and decided I could help out too. I took care of the gardening at the shelter. Made it a nice place outside, you know, a peaceful place. When Mary and her little one came there, I'd already heard what happened to Pike. My sister still lives in the old neighbourhood; she told me. So I put two and two together, you know." Rita waited for a moment then asked, "You want me to keep goin'?"

Keely nodded.

"Mary and I got to talkin'. I told her about what happened to my Candy," Rita said.

Candace blushed and looked away.

"Sorry, Candy. It was a long time ago, you know. Anyway, Mary knew about Zander, too. Guess her husband told her 'bout his part in takin' Zander to see Moreau and Pike that day after school. Then I saw the news. Moreau had some free apartments. I knew it meant that anyone who turned Mary in would get a free place to live. So I kept an eye out for Mary and the baby. They were gonna come and stay with me 'cause it was only a matter of time before Moreau or one of his people showed up. And he did. Walked right past me after he shot that one over there." Rita turned to Keely. "Sorry, it happened so fast, there was nothin' I could do."

Keely shrugged and the movement caused her to grimace. "How come Moreau didn't see you?"

"I was workin' at the corner of the hedge. I ducked behind it when Dee Dee opened the gate for him."

"Dee Dee?" Lane asked.

"The one he shot in the backyard. She was collecting on Moreau's offer of a free apartment. Anyway, I got mad at myself for standing around. I've been mad for a long time about what he did to Candy. I went to the side of the house. I could see what was going on from there. Kev had his back to me and was pointin' his gun at Mary. So I took my shovel and swung it like an axe. The blood splattered on my face. After that I picked up the gun and pointed it at him." Rita looked at Lane as if asking him whether she should continue.

"Who called the ambulance?" Lane asked.

"I did," Mary said. "I picked up Joshua and went around to the front door and inside to use the phone. Rita stayed outside and watched Kev. When I came back outside, Moreau was lying on his side, kind of panting and shivering."

The lawyer, Ms. Scott, said, "Candace insisted that all three stories be told at one time, so that the entire series of events could be put into context."

Lane frowned.

Candace asked, "Is there a problem?"

"When you examined Keely's wound, you knew that Moreau would go for a head shot and the heart. How did you know that?" Lane asked.

The lawyer grabbed Candace's forearm. Candace shook it

off. "He used to take me target shooting. He bragged about what a good shot he was and that only one shot was usually necessary. But his backup was the heart shot. He used to say that life on the streets was hard."

"Why were you involved with him?" Lane asked.

Candace looked at her aunt then at Lane. "I was in love with him — or, at least, that's what I thought at the time."

"Who's paying for the lawyer?" Keely asked.

"Me," Candace said.

"How?" Keely asked.

"I've been putting money away for years. There aren't very many opportunities to spend money in the places where I work," Candace said.

chapter 16

"Fibre here."

"Any news on the family front?" Lane asked.

"We found out yesterday. It's two boys and a girl!" Fibre said.

"Ummm," Lane said.

"It is amazing, isn't it? And Gaia has agreed to live next door in my duplex. That way I can help when the babies are born because she wants to continue working. I might even take a leave of absence."

"That's wonderful news."

"It wouldn't have happened without your advice."

"Any news on the Moreau investigation?" Lane asked.

"Of course."

His voice just went monotone again. Amazing, Lane thought.

"Here it is. DNA evidence puts Jessica and Matt in the apartment along with the accused abductor. Also, the investigation of the women's shelter crime scene is completed. If you want, I will leave a copy of the report with my secretary. The investigation of Moreau's residence turned up a copy of the movie you were asking about. It's an amateur production with a young woman and a younger Kevin Moreau." Fibre cleared his throat.

"Is it of any value to the investigation?" Lane asked.

"I don't believe so. Would you like to pick it up when you come for the crime scene report?"

"Yes, please," Lane said.

"I will do that right now so that it will be ready whenever you arrive." Fibre hung up.

chapter 17

"You're sure you're feeling well enough?" Lane asked.

"Will you stop it? I mean, yes, I'm still sore. And yes, I'm having flashbacks. But I want to do this. It's a good thing to do. You know, move forward." Keely sat in the passenger seat. Lane drove north and west down into the river valley.

"How's your family doing?" Lane asked.

"Mom's fine. Saadiq is fine. Dylan keeps bringing food and flowers over. My dad, well, he'll never change." Keely took a deep, careful breath.

"Saadiq sure helped us out when it came to finding Matt and Jessica. He's got a real network of friends. I don't know how I'll ever be able to pay back that debt." Lane guided the car over the bridge. Underneath, the highway traffic headed west toward the mountains.

"Don't worry, he still thinks he owes you. Remember how you helped me out after the explosion and the other day when you told me to wear a vest? He still thinks he has a ways to go to even things out."

"Does your dad think he's in my debt?" Lane smiled.

"As a matter of fact, he does, sort of. Well, with him it's always complicated. He respects you, and he thinks you're an abomination." Keely looked sideways at Lane. "What exactly are you up to? And are you sure you want me over to your place for lunch tomorrow?"

"Yes, Arthur says we all need to get together and celebrate. You have Candace's address?" Lane asked.

Keely pulled the envelope up from where it sat next to her feet. "Take a right here. Keep heading west."

They entered a residential district. In less than five minutes, they parked in front of a house whose yard backed against a hill that reached all the way up to the Trans-Canada Highway.

Lane waited for Keely to ease out of the Chev. She had the envelope tucked in the crook of her right arm.

As they walked up the sidewalk that bisected the front yard, Lane said, "You take this one."

Keely nodded and knocked on the front door.

Candace was dressed in jeans and a T-shirt when she opened the door. "Detectives?"

Keely said, "We have something for you." She held up the envelope.

Candace invited them into a front room where one wall was devoted to pictures of exotic and remote locations from around the world.

"Amazing photos." Lane moved closer to look at a picture of a jungle where the mist had settled in the valleys. It made the hills look like islands in a sea of white. "Where was this one taken?"

"Fraser's Hill in Malaysia. Woke up one morning, got the camera out and took that one." Candace sat down in an armchair. "My mom's gone to work so we can talk. Am I going to be charged?"

"We don't know for sure. That decision is in the hands of the Crown." Lane sat down opposite Candace. "Off the record, we've been told that charges are unlikely."

Keely handed the envelope to Candace and then sat down on the couch.

"What's this?" Candace asked.

"A home movie found at Moreau's house. The person in charge of forensics says it's of no evidentiary value and was the only copy found in the home." Keely then lifted her left arm to rest it on the back of the couch.

Candace frowned, opened the envelope and then closed it again.

Keely pointed at her partner. "We thought you might, you know, want to burn it, crush it, flush it, whatever."

"All three, perhaps?" Candace asked.

Keely shrugged, then winced. "Whatever you decide."

Lane saw that Candace's face was turning red. He said, "You should know that you will receive official word from the Crown within a week."

Candace put the envelope on an end table.

A child wearing black pajamas entered the room. "Mummy?"

"Femi." Candace went to pick the boy up. He tucked his curly black hair under her chin. She sat back down. Femi looked at the detectives with frank curiosity. His brown eyes flicked from Keely to Lane.

"Hello," Lane said.

Femi nestled closer to his mother.

"How old are you?" Keely asked.

Femi held up two fingers. "Three."

"I've been thinking it may be time for Femi and me to come home," Candace said. "A boy needs to know he has a family."

"A boy certainly does," Lane said.

"Congratulations," Candace said to Keely.

"Thank you." Her face turned red.

Lane looked at Keely's left hand to see that she was again wearing an engagement ring.

chapter 18

Lane rolled over in bed when Arthur opened the bedroom door. "What time is it?"

Arthur sat down on the bed next to him. "After eleven."

Lane looked at the curtains and saw the sun shining in. *Must be morning.*

"Did you ever think that when Matt arrived on our doorstep we would live through something like this?"

Lane sat up and shook his head. He reached out and held Arthur's hand. "We make a pretty good team, the four of us."

"Five. The team keeps getting bigger." He let go of Lane's hand and stood up. "Erinn and Cam are here, and the kids. You're missing the show." Arthur hesitated before going to the door. "Do you think we'll survive this?"

"What do you mean?"

"There's not much time for you and me anymore." Arthur went out the door and downstairs.

Lane heard Jessica speak. Then he heard Cam Harper's voice. When he came down the stairs, he saw Harper watching his daughter. Jessica was sitting next to Matt on the living room floor, and he was reading a book to her while she pointed at the pictures. Arthur, Erinn and Christine were in conversation on the couch. As Lane stepped into the living room, Daniel handed him a cup of coffee.

Lane took a sip. "Perfect. Thank you."

Daniel sat on the arm of the couch next to Christine.

Harper looked at his watch and smiled. "It's almost noon."

Lane said, "You're kidding."

"You slept for almost fourteen hours!" Christine said.

Harper motioned Lane over and spoke quietly. "Robert Rowe died last night. One of the bullets hit his liver. He went into a coma and didn't regain consciousness."

Lane nodded. "I've been thinking about something Saadiq said about our society needing people to wipe tables and sell cheap shit."

"I don't understand," Harper said.

Lane shrugged. "I didn't think you would because that's not the way your mind works."

Harper said, "I was thinking about what would have happened to Matt and Christine if you and Arthur hadn't taken them in."

"You're thinking about the difference between a drive-by and driving into a card shop?" Lane asked.

"Something like that," Harper said.

Erinn took Lane's elbow. "You know that Matt of yours is a wonder. Jessica still thinks she went on a trip with him. He made the whole thing into a game." She kissed Lane on the cheek.

"What's that for?" Lane asked.

"You figure it out," Erinn said.

Arthur looked out the window. "Lane! Answer the door. Keely's here and she's got Dylan with her."

Lane went to the front door and saw Keely and Dylan smiling at each other as they met at the sidewalk side of the car. The back seat was filled with luggage, blankets and towels. *They're on their way. What will I do now?*

ACKNOWLEDGMENTS

Bruce and Shameem, thank you.

Again, thanks to Tony Bidulka and Wayne Gunn.

Thank you to John for the police procedural advice.

Mary, Alex and Sebi, thanks for the suggestions and feedback.

Ben and Al, thanks for the advice on untraceable telephones.

Doug, Paul, Matt, Tiiu, Natalie and Leslie, thanks for all that you do.

Thanks to creative writers at Nickle, Bowness, Lord Beaverbrook, Alternative, Forest Lawn and Queen Elizabeth.

Sharon, Karma, Luke, Ben, Meredith, Indiana and Ella: that is new!

In 2004, NeWest Press published Garry Ryan's first Detective Lane novel, *Queen's Park*. The second, *The Lucky Elephant Restaurant*, won a 2007 Lambda Literary Award. NeWest has since published four more titles in the series: *A Hummingbird Dance*, *Smoked*, *Malabarista* and *Foxed*. In 2009, Ryan was awarded Calgary's Freedom of Expression Award. In 2012 he began a second series with the historical fiction novel *Blackbirds*, also published by NeWest Press.